SI~~~~~~~~~~~~~~~~
KANGAROO

By Sally Squires

Skin of the Kangaroo

SKIN OF THE KANGAROO

by Sally Squires

© Copyright Sally Squires 2014
For further information:
G'Day Inc
PO Box 37126
Honolulu HI 96837
USA
email: GDay1717@hotmail.com
ssquires1717@gmail.com

Copies of this book are available:
www.amazon.com
www.createspace.com
or from the publisher

Skin of the Kangaroo

Dedicated to Tifu and Casey

In Memory of Shirley

Thanks to Maryann Barnett

NOTE ON SPELLING:

As the story is set in Australia and the USA I have used Australian spelling for those sections and US spelling for the US sections. Occasionally I have used my own spelling.

AUSTRALIA 1957

The desert sand holds a certain magic that tells a windswept story if you just care to listen and believe. The magic can be felt through the soles of the feet of traditional Aboriginal dancers in the outback as they dance the kangaroo dance. It's a magic that can unite souls across an ocean. It's a magic that can bring heartache too. It's a magic that goes beyond class, beyond race, beyond any differences between people. It's a magic beyond time.

The desert sand wove its magic on Troy (5), his sister Sabia (3) and their mother Rose long ago when the world was a different place. It was the darker side of that magic that scooped up Troy and Sabia and Rose that day weaving a new kind of life for the three of them. Until the desert sand spoke that day Troy and Sabia had been happily playing together as they always did in a series of bush games that they knew. Free, unfettered and alive under the brilliant ocean-coloured sky of West Australia in a time of magic, Troy and Sabia share a 70,000 year heritage. It courses through their blood like a river of knowledge. Inherent in their Aboriginal genes are the stories of the Dreamtime – the unwritten history of Australian Aborigines' past handed down through the generations like a map from the stars, a unique history binding them to their ancestors.

On that day in that year of innocence some of the spirits of those ancient ancestors may have been watching from behind the gum trees or sitting on top of the red, hot rocks as Troy chased Sabia through the spinifex. They were both very adept at dodging the spiky white plants. Laughing, Sabia turned to see where her brother was and fell down on the hot, red desert sand. Troy caught up to her, scooped her up and brushed off the sand. Sabia hugged him and smiled. She loved her brother fiercely. He was her other world.

Growing up free in the bush, they knew the secret places and one of their favourites was the waterlily pond at Millstream which was a natural spring in the desert arising from the bowels of the driest continent on earth.

Swimming was just like breathing to them. The soft velvet shallows of the waterlily pond were a daily haunt and the backdrop to many of their games. Sabia jumped from Troy's shoulders between two lily plants into the water. Suddenly she screamed: "Snake! Troy! Snake!" She stared at something just behind Troy. He turned around and picked up something out of the water. He teased her with the dark shape. "It's gunna get you but I'll save you, little sister." Troy banged the dark shape on his head. Sabia was horrified. "Nah! Not a snake, just a piece of wood." Sabia smiled. She was used to Troy and his tricks. This wasn't the first time he had teased her about her fears but Troy always leaves Sabia in no doubt about how much he loves his sister. Later, as if to pay her back for teasing her, he starts to carve the piece of wood into a goanna for her. He knows that Sabia is aware that goannas eat snakes so he feels that the wooden talisman may take away some of her fears. Unknown to the children – or to their mother, Rose – at that very moment a darker threat to them had been unleashed that day. Not a snake as such but definitely snake-like intentions as two men in dark suits left a city office. Their movements echoed each other as they turned in unison and got into identical black, shiny cars.

As the noon sun paused in the brilliant sky, Rose was teaching the children how to catch a goanna, which was sunning itself on a rock. Creeping up on it silently and motioning for them to follow her, she held her fingers to her lips so they knew not to make a sound. Suddenly, Rose pounced and the goanna was caught.

Later, as the lengthening shadows touch the rocks around Python Pool, Rose lights a fire between her fire rocks. She shows Troy and Sabia how to skin the goanna. They watch her carefully slide the knife in under the skin, turning the body as she goes so the skin comes off cleanly in one piece. Then she hands the goanna to Troy who expertly passes a stick down through the body, placing it carefully over the hot coals. As darkness descends, Troy cuts pieces of the goanna and passes them to his sister who chews happily. This is Sabia's favourite time of the day. She knows that soon she will be lying by the campfire with her mother on one side and her brother on the other side of her. She feels their strength as she lies between them. She knows that she is safe from all of her childhood fears. Nothing and no-one can "get her" during the night.

Dawn breaks softly lighting the way for Rose and the children to walk to the lilypond. Rose shushes them as she sees two kangaroos on the grass. They watch quietly and then, as if in response to a silent signal, the kangaroos hop away.

Meanwhile the two black cars continue their snake-like journey north on Great Northern Highway towards the turnoff to Millstream. The drivers of the cars are dark shapes on a mission.

In contrast to the menace of the moving cars, stretching out on both sides of the road is a colourful carpet of wildflowers. The paperlike flowers have adapted to the harshness of the West Australian climate where rain is a sometime thing but nature needs its flowers to be fertilized so it paints the dry desert sand with these carpets of colour every year to attract the brilliantly patterned butterflies and bees that drift on slight breezes from flower to flower, flowers which last for months because of their paper petals in a desperate attempt to attract the attention of the insects.

Rose, Troy and Sabia swim in the lilypond unaware that this will be the last time they will swim together for thirty years.

As dusk starts to creep its tawny fingers over the landscape the two black cars reach the turnoff, their drivers both slow down and turn in the direction of where Sabia and Troy are playing happily in the sand.

Troy has a toy, yellow tip truck. He makes engine noises as he pushes it through the sand. As he drives the truck, Sabia fills it with sand. The red desert sand slips through her fingers into the tray of the truck in just the same way as the sand slips through an hourglass. Suddenly a noise disturbs the children. They see the black tyres of the cars roll through the red desert sand towards them. Two men get out but, crouched down on the sand as they are, all the children can see are big, black, shiny shoes. The men are smiling. They bend down. Their faces almost touch the children's faces.

Troy picks up his truck, sand cascades onto the ancient, desert floor. Prompted by some unknown instinct, he opens up his string dillybag lying near his feet and grabs for the wooden goanna which he pushes into the stubby, fat fingers of his sister. It is not quite finished as Troy wanted to carve some special markings on the tail but his instinct tells him to give it to Sabia now. She clings to it, not looking at the goanna but looking into the men's smiling faces. Neither Sabia nor Troy are smiling, their serious faces flag their instinct that something is wrong. Each man now holds a struggling child. As the cars drive away, the two children peer agonizingly out of the windows of the cars....... separate cars. They are crying but the windows are wound up so their pain is silent.

Rose, who was too far away to stop the theft of her children, runs down the road after them crying out: "My babies! My babies!" She had dreaded this day ever coming and now her worst fears have been realized. Rose had taken the children into the bush camp soon after she had heard about the children being taken away from their mothers. Terrifying scenes had been played out across the country as children of Aboriginal mothers had been forcibly removed from their parents and families "for their own good." Their move into the bush had been the second escape for Rose and the children. The constant beatings Rose had suffered at the hands of the children's father had led her to escape from her family group when Sabia was a baby and Troy a toddler. So the bush and the animals and birds had served as family to the three of them bringing them closer to nature and giving them a resilience that city bred folk often do not have.

AUSTRALIA 1987

It is thirty years since the day of the abduction and Sabia is now a confident young lawyer making her mark in the city of Perth. On this day she is representing a young defendant and arguing his case before a woman magistrate.

"Your Honour, this is a clear case of discrimination and provocation by the police. My client was simply on an errand for his mother when he was stopped by the police for no reason. Naturally a young man is going to question their motives. We agree his language was intemperate. He should not have used the terms he used."

Both Sabia and the magistrate look across at the defendant, Terry, an Aboriginal youth about 14 years old. He looks embarrassed. Catching the magistrate's eye, Sabia continues: "Regardless of that, to charge him with resisting arrest when the police had no grounds for arresting him is unacceptable. I ask that these charges - disorderly conduct and resisting arrest - be dismissed."

The magistrate leans forward, looking at Terry but addressing her remarks to Sabia. "Ms Malone, I have to agree with you. In the light of testimonials by several character witnesses, your client's school record and the fact that he has never been in trouble before, I am going to dismiss these charges."

Terry smiles at the prosecutor.

Gathering up her papers and packing her briefcase, Sabia says: "Come on I'll drive you home."

"Thank you Miss, I thought they had me."

Sabia and Terry wait for the lift. Her briefcase is jam-packed with papers. The lift doors open. It too is packed. People can hardly move. As the lift reaches the lobby, everyone rushes to leave. Sabia is pushed aside. She struggles to stay on her feet. In the process she drops her briefcase. The contents spill onto the floor. Terry helps her pick up her court papers. Underneath one of the files is the little wooden goanna. Terry picks it up. "You got kids?" he asks as he hands her the goanna. Sabia shakes her head as she tucks it back into her briefcase. She answers the unasked question. "It's sort of a good luck charm."

In the car Terry watches her as she drives. He is curious about her. "So, wher'ya from?"

Sabia is not sure what he means exactly. "I live here."

"I mean which mob do you belong to?"

Sabia debates with herself whether she should answer such personal questions from a client. "I don't know."

"You don't know where you're from? Are you one of the stolen ones?"

"I don't know."

"So you don't know who your family is? Don't you want to find out? Me ...... I've got nine brothers and sisters. Geez! Sometimes I wish I didn't know who my family was! But other times it's all right. On Sundays, Mum...God, she's tough! She makes us all this big lunch. All the cousins and aunties and uncles come. They get drunk and tell stories. It's great. Uncle Sammy plays guitar. He's teachin' me. And Auntie Mavis - she's a card shark. She's teachin' me some wicked tricks."

Sabia takes a quick look at how animated Terry has become when he talks about his family. "Sounds nice," she says. "I guess I've never felt the need to find out where I'm from. My father......."

"Your white father....," Terry butts in.

"My father. He's dead now. He was a good man. And my mother - she's a good woman." And Sabia hopes that will be the end of his questions but Terry is not to be dissuaded.

"They're not your real parents, not your family," he prods.

Sabia is determined to put him right. "They're family alright. Family's not just a question of blood. It's feelings. Feelings and commitment." Suddenly a sharp pain rips through Sabia's stomach. She grabs at her stomach and the car lurches towards the middle of the road. Terry reaches across her lap, grabs the steering wheel and corrects the direction of the car.

"OWWW!" Sabia clutches her stomach. Terry is concerned.

"Are you alright?" he asks as she brings the car to a stop.

"I will be in a few minutes. The pain usually only lasts a few minutes."

"Maybe you should see a doc," says Terry.

The next day Sabia decides to take Terry's advice. She has been suffering these intermittent pain attacks for some weeks but her workload meant she had kept postponing any visits to doctors. As Doctor Kelligan finishes examining her, he says: "I'm sorry, Ms Malone but I can't find anything wrong."

She is puzzled. "When I get these cramps, I can't even stand up."

"Perhaps it's something you've eaten that doesn't agree with you." Doctor Kelligan hands her a referral. "Just to be on the safe side I'm going to refer you to a specialist. Maybe I am missing something."

ROSE – AUSTRALIA

A thousand miles north of where Sabia is getting into her car outside the doctor's office, someone remembers that it is thirty years ago since her two children were taken away from her.

Every year, at the same time that Troy and Sabia were taken away, Rose comes back to camp at Python Pool. The pool is a sacred Aboriginal place. The spirits and whispers of the Dreamtime stories infuse it with a special atmosphere that even a first time visitor would be affected by. The jagged, dried-blood red stone cliffs swoop down into the turquoise green water which is such a strange colour that the whole scene looks as if it has been painted by some over-active Andy Warhol.

Rose walks down to the pool. Even her steps show a reverence for this sacred place. She scoops up water in her hands and blows some of it into the air. A tiny rainbow forms in the droplets. Satisfied that she has permission of the spirit people, she scoops up more water in her billycan then carries it back to the fire she has lit in the rocks. Carefully she places the billycan so that it balances over the fire. While the water boils she throws a fishing line into the pool as she has done so many times before. She hasn't given up hope that her children will one day return. One day, she tells herself, I will fish here again with Troy and Sabia but time is running out for Rose and she knows only too well that her body is ready to give up even though her spirit is still strong.

TROY – USA

On the other side of the world, Troy walks through the front door of a downtown hospital in one of America's cities. He gets into an elevator to the 3rd floor Children's Ward clutching a purple bunny. Walking over to one of the beds he sits down on Suzy's bed. She has her left arm bandaged and Troy has bandaged the left arm of the bunny to look like her wound. He hands the bandaged bunny to Suzy. "There you are. Now bunny's arm will heal just like yours." Suzy smiles. "Tell me a story, Troy. Then I promise, I promise, I'll go to sleep."

Troy lays the bunny down on the pillow next to Suzy and picks up her good hand as he starts the story. He strokes her hand. "Once upon a time there was a boy and a girl - a brother and sister. They were playing at the beach when a big wind came blowing along the sand. They stood up to see where the wind had come from but it was so strong that it almost blew them over. They held hands to stop themselves from being blown away, but it was no good. The wind just got stronger and stronger. Then it started to rain and their hands got all wet and slippery, so slippery that their fingers slid out of each other's grasp. The boy was blown one way and his sister was blown the other way. They lost sight of each other and began to call out their names but no-one heard them because the wind was so loud. All of a sudden, the wind stopped and then the sun came out and a beautiful rainbow made a perfect arch across the sky. The boy looked at the rainbow and the girl looked at the rainbow. And each one could see the other one at the opposite ends of the rainbow. They waved at each other, they were so happy to see each other. And they began to walk towards each other. Finally they met in the very middle of the rainbow in the sky."

As he finishes the story, Troy reaches towards Suzy and lightly pinches her nose. "And if you look up into the sky and see a rainbow, you'll see that brother and sister holding hands and smiling at each other. Just see if you don't."

Suzy jumps out of bed and runs to the window. It is dark outside. "Troy, there's no rainbow."

Troy picks her up and carries her back to bed. As he tucks her in he says: "But there will be. You just keep looking. There's always a rainbow."

A nurse comes into the room. Smiling at Troy she says: "Don't you want to have children of your own? You're so good with them."

"Maybe, some day."

The nurse fluffs up Suzy's pillows. "They really look forward to you coming in here."

"Glad to do it," says Troy as he leaves.

SABIA – AUSTRALIA

Summer evenings settle on the Perth skyline like a blanket of butterflies. The yachts are out on the river for another evening of twilight sailing as Sabia and her adoptive mother, Madeline, trawl for prawns (shrimp) in the Swan River. Madeline holds both ends of the trawling net while Sabia is sitting on the riverbank putting on her sandshoes. She laces up the second one, bounces to her feet taking one end of the net from her mother. "Right, let's go." The two women wade into the river about 20 feet apart. They walk straight out into the river until the water is up to their necks. Then they turn and walk towards each other, slowly. They walk slowly so they will catch the prawns in their net. If they walk too fast they won't catch anything.

A little later the sun has set and it is dark. The two women have the net spread out on the riverbank. By the light of two hurricane lamps they sort out their catch. The prawns jump about in the net as they pick them out and drop them into a bucket. Sabia finishes picking out the prawns as Madeline gets a fire going. She throws the last of the prawns into the bucket and then helps Madeline place it carefully on the rocks over the fire. The prawns cook quickly and Sabia scoops them out into big bowls. There is a companionable silence between them while they work. It's only broken by an Australian adjective or two as a prawn is accidentally dropped into the sand. After their feast the two women share a beer. Four cans of Swan Lager catch the light from the hurricane lamps. Sabia is in a pensive mood. She lies back on the blanket they are sharing looking up at the stars. "Didn't they even tell you who my parents were?"

Madeline is a bit surprised at Sabia's question as she's never enquired before about her background or family. "Back then the government didn't tell us anything."

"Didn't you want to know who I was?"

"I didn't care. I thought you were the most beautiful little girl I'd ever seen. Wouldn't have mattered to me if you'd flown in from Mars. I'd wanted my own daughter for so many years. Ken and me, we'd just about given up. Couldn't believe it when we got the letter." Sabia squeezes her Mum's hand. "Thanks Mum."

"For what?"

"Everything. You've been the best mother anyone could have."

"And you've been the best daughter any mother could have." Madeline starts to laugh, dropping prawn shells all over the blanket. "You were so funny when you were little. You might be playing in your sandpit or even in bed and suddenly you'd stand up and say: "I am Sabia!"

Sabia chuckles.

"When we first got you we thought about changing your name - Ken wanted to name you after his mother, Edith."

Sabia grimaces. "Eeeh - thank goodness you didn't let him."

"Oh, it wasn't me. It was you – 'I am Sabia'. That's all you would say for about a year."

The next day Sabia is still thinking about their prawn feast and how lucky she is to have such a wonderful mother as she pulls into the driveway of Dr Kelligan's office.

As she sits down, the doctor pulls out a report and letter from the specialist. "It's not good news I'm afraid Miss Malone."

"Just tell me Doctor. Don't sugar coat it."

"You have leukaemia."

"Leukaemia?" Sabia is disbelieving.

Doctor Kelligan is always troubled when he has to advise a patient of serious news. "It's early stage. If we can get a bone marrow donor, we may be able to catch it in time."

"A donor?" asks Sabia.

"A relative would be the best bet, but we'd have to test them first to see if they're a match. Do you have any relatives who would be willing to be tested?"

"None that I know of," said Sabia.

"Your mother?"

"I'm adopted."

"Oh. No-one else?"

"I don't think so."

After receiving such devastating news, Sabia sits down on a park bench next to the doctor's office to try to absorb the doctor's words. She feels numb. For months she had put off visiting a doctor hoping that if she ignored the pains they would just go away. Slowly the doctor's words sink in and she begins to realize that she must make a plan about what to do next. She is a great planner. It is the easiest way she knows to overcome any hurdles or challenges that life throws at her. To help her focus she fishes in her bag and gets out a pen and paper. "Find a donor" she writes at the top of the page. Then HOW in big letters. She starts to list some steps of action she can take. 1. Adoption agency. 2. Library records. 3. Newspaper reports. Then she runs out of ideas but finally she writes: 4. Court documents. Surely there must be some record of her adoption, she thinks.

The next day Sabia starts the search for her blood relatives. Madeline remembered the agency through which the adoption was carried out so she has a starting point. It took determined persistence by Sabia. She had had to be very insistent with the manager's assistant before she could even get into his office. She is now seated opposite the agency manager. He tries to look interested in what she is asking him, but it is obvious he would rather be somewhere else. Sabia's questions are making him uncomfortable. "I'm sorry, Miss Malone, but we don't have any records that far back. I can't give you any information about your family."

Sabia doesn't believe him. She leans across his desk towards him and he instantly leans back. "But you're talking about my family, **my** family, not yours, not the government's, not some bureaucrat's family. I want to know about my family. For thirty years you've kept me in the dark. This is not your secret to keep."

"Believe me, I do understand."

Sabia is angry. She pulls up the sleeve of her blouse. She waves her arm under the nose of the bureaucrat. "You think that because my skin is darker than yours, I don't have any feelings, don't you?"

"It's not that, Miss Malone. I sympathize with your situation but there's nothing I can do."

"Well there's something I can do, I can subpoena your records."

"You don't understand, those records were destroyed in a fire twenty years ago."

"Someone must remember, even after all these years."

"I'm sorry. That was before my time here. There isn't anyone here from back then. It's a long time. You're talking about something that happened thirty years ago."

"Something that happened! Something that happened! Yeah, something happened alright."

"The records just don't exist anymore."

"Well that's just lovely, isn't it? I'm talking about a life and death situation and you're telling me 'something happened'. I'll say something happened. I was ...." She storms out.

A headache starts to form as Sabia comes out of the front door of the adoption office. As she walks down the street to her car she sees two children playing in the park opposite. She walks across the road to watch them for a few moments. As she watches the children play, she suddenly has a snatch of a memory of playing with a young boy. She sees his hand pushing a little yellow truck through the sand. She tries to look up into his face but the memory fades before she can see his face. She takes one last look at the children playing and walks off. Her headache begins to lift.

Sabia's quest into her past takes her into a newspaper office where she checks back copies of the paper that are stored in their library catalogues. She looks for newspaper stories that have anything to do with the treatment of Aboriginal children, then checks through the birth columns of 1954, the year of her birth, but she can't find any relevant information. Sabia had always known that she was adopted. Madeline and Ken had told her the truth when she was four or five. They told her she was special and that she had been chosen by them to be their own daughter. She'd never thought much about it when she was growing up. She had always had so much love and care from her parents – as she thought of them – that she had never had a doubt that they looked upon her the same as they would for a naturally born child. She'd always felt special because of the way they had treated her and she had had everything a child could want. They'd both encouraged her to go to university, though neither of them had had that opportunity. She realized that she was luckier than a lot of other young people growing up and she had been grateful for that. Though she had taken her studies seriously she had lived a fairly carefree life – until now. She was devoted to both her parents and she was just as devoted to her studies and to her career. She felt that she owed them a debt of gratitude and so she had led a quiet life focusing on her career at the expense of a social life. She also felt a great obligation to her legal clients and so spent more hours than most lawyers would on preparing for each case. Sabia felt that men would divert her from her focus and she had a secret desire to one day sit on the bench as a judge though she would never admit that not even to Madeline, her mother. Though she had not thought much about her birth parents, she had always believed that they had given her up for adoption for their own reasons and so she had not felt betrayed by them. Quite the opposite, she was grateful that they had realized that they could not cope and so she had had a life which was perhaps better than the one she might have had. Of course she had heard and read stories about the "stolen generations" of Aboriginal children being taken from their natural parents but she had never put herself in that picture before. She wonders why she has not been more curious about her past. She has a vague feeling that she has let down someone because she has not been more active in her search for her original family and is angry at herself because if she had carried out such a search already she would have vital information which could help her now that she needs a donor to.........maybe save her life.

TROY – USA

Unknown to Sabia her possible donor is thousands of miles away across the other side of the world. Troy is in a downtown gym in the boxing ring sparring with Jason, a young boxer. It is obvious Jason has talent. They finish sparring, both remove their headgear as they get out of the ring. While Troy is talking to Jason, Keesha comes into the gym and waits near them. She is a friend of Jason. Troy continues with his lesson. "Remember to keep your guard up, Jason. Don't ever give your opponent a chance to get in under your guard."

"I'll remember."

Troy turns to Keesha. "Did you call your mother like you promised?"

"Give me time," says Keesha with a cheeky grin.

Troy takes some money out of his pocket. "Here. Call her. Tell her you're all right."

"I will. Don't worry about money. I know a phone that doesn't need money."

Troy gives her a serious look. "No games."

"No games. This phone just likes the sound of my voice."

Troy hands her the money. Keesha hesitates. "I told you I don't need it."

"It's for food. You're losing weight."

"Hey, I'm supposed to be. I'm going to be a model."

"Great, but you still need to eat."

Keesha smiles. "What are you, my father?"

"A friend. Everyone needs a friend."

"So, friend. I'll call my mother...and I'll eat."

"Promise?"

"Promise and hope to die!"

"Don't say that."

Keesha starts to walk away. "Later. Come on Jason."

SABIA – AUSTRALIA

Sabia is all business as she pulls up in her car outside the court. She gathers her briefcase and is just about to get out of the car when she is hit by a wave of pain. She closes her eyes against the pain and in her mind's eye sees an unfamiliar scene. It is as if she is sitting on a hill overlooking a river. There is no-one else around. It is afternoon - about 4.30pm. A flock of white cockatoos flies languidly along the river, then they turn as if hearing some invisible command and find seating spots on the branches of fallen gum trees that reach out into the river. They dip their beaks into the river and drink. In Sabia's daydream this scene is quickly replaced by another. She is standing on the shore looking across a pool to red, high cliffs. A snake slithers down the cliffs and drops into the water. It leaves a trail of displaced water as it disappears into the pool.

TROY – USA

Half a world away another snake slithers around a tank inside the pet shop where Troy works as the manager. The shop is full of bright colors from the screeching parrots in cages. Among the riotous and colorful scene, Troy is almost impossible to see as he bends down to pour food into the feeding trough of a cage of white mice. There is a brightly colored parrot perched on his shoulder. As he straightens up, the parrot starts pecking at his hair. Troy rubs his head.

"Charlie stop that! I don't have fleas and I'm not your dinner."

Charlie the parrot answers him. "Not your dinner! Not your dinner!"

Troy's boss, Maryanne Marquette, comes out of the back of the shop. She has a birthday cake on which are 35 candles. Troy senses some movement behind him and turns around.

Maryanne sings: "Happy Birthday to you, Happy Birthday to you, Happy Birthday dear Troy, Happy Birthday to you."

Troy is surprised – pleased, but surprised. "How did you know it was my birthday?"

Maryanne grins. "A little bird told me."

Troy looks around at all the birds and, in an Al Capone voice, says: "All right, you guys. 'Fess up. Which one of you squealed?" The birds are all squealing. As he eats some cake Troy reaches up and gives some to Charlie who is still perched on his shoulder. "While you're here, Maryanne, I'll take the dog for a walk. Thanks for the cake." Charlie starts swaying on Troy's shoulder: "Walk the dog! Walk the dog!" Gently Troy takes Charlie off his shoulder and puts him on a perch. Charlie protests by squawking. "Not you Charlie. You're not a dog." Charlie is not to be denied. He starts doing dog impressions. "Bark! Bark! Woof! Woof!" Troy ignores him as he buckles up his dog's leash. "Come on, Tiger."

Later that night Troy tosses and turns in bed. He is suffering from a nightmare. It is a recurrent nightmare that he has not been able to blot out. The roar of the shooting seems so close that his eardrums hurt. Once again he relives the tortuous scene that has haunted him almost every day of his adult life. Suddenly he jerks awake. Tiger, who has been sleeping on the floor next to his bed, also wakes. "Come on Tiger, walk."

Deep shadows seem to follow Troy and Tiger as they walk the deserted night-time streets of the city. Deep shadows hide the secret movements of drug deals, illicit sex and things better left unknown. Troy is used to these streets. Walking Tiger is his way of coping with the nightmares. His is a private world. He has never discussed the nightmares with anyone. They have made him withdraw into himself even

more than he would have naturally after his parents –
his adoptive parents – were killed in a car accident
when he was 16. Since then he has been on his own,
building a wall around his emotions to insulate
himself from some of the darker aspects of life.

SABIA – AUSTRALIA

Meanwhile Sabia has decided to do some lateral
thinking. She has always been a believer in a person's
instincts and, realizing that she needs some kind of
miracle to help her find the information she needs to
help her fight the battle of her life, she is in a map
shop looking through the maps. She picks up one and
looks at it, discards it, then picks up another one. The
maps are of different regions of the state of West
Australia. Finally she has about 10 maps stacked on
the counter. The shop assistant rings up the sale:
"You're gunna be travelling," she says.

"Maybe." Sabia shrugs.

Later that evening Sabia is visiting Madeline. She
has all the maps spread over the kitchen table while
Madeline is making coffee. "I'm sorry I haven't been
much help," says Madeline.

"What do you mean you haven't been much help?
You had the tests done to see if you could be my
donor," says Sabia giving Madeline a hug.

"Well I certainly wish I'd been a match. That was
the least I could do. You know I would do anything
for you. What are you going to do with all those
maps?"

"Not really sure," says Sabia, taking the coffee.
"But I thought I might spread out these maps and look
at each one and see if I'm attracted to one of them
more than the others. Maybe that will give me a clue.

Perhaps my instincts will tell me where I come from....came from." Sabia decides to do her research methodically so she arranges the maps from north to south of the state of West Australia. The first map is of the Kimberley region and the very north of the state. After a thorough going over of the map she reluctantly folds it up and then moves on to the next map of the Pilbara region. She runs her hand over it then opens it up to where there are photographs of scenes from the local area. She turns white. "My God!"

"What is it, Sabia? Are you all right?" Madeline is concerned.

Sabia points to one of the photos on the map. "That's what I saw. That's what I saw."

"Saw? What? When?" Madeline is puzzled. Sabia points to two of the photographs on the map. They are the same scenes that she saw in her daydream. "The other day. I was just getting out of my car when I got those stomach cramps again and I closed my eyes to try to block out the pain. Sometimes that helps. Anyhow, I saw those two photographs. Well I saw those two places. Exactly like that."

JASON – USA

It is a cold night in Jason's mother, Cheyenne's apartment. Cheyenne is in bed. She has been sick for several weeks and Jason is her only caregiver. He is heating up some soup on the stove as she lies there watching him. Cheyenne wants Jason to contact his father but Jason is adamant. "I'm not gonna try to find him. He doesn't want to find us." Cheyenne is just as stubborn. "He'll have to help now that I'm sick."

Jason pours the soup into a bowl, gets some

crackers and puts them carefully on a tray which he brings over to his mother's bedside. Helping her to sit up he says: "I can take care of you. I'm grown."

Cheyenne is proud of her son but she does not want to be a burden on his young life. "Fifteen is not grown up enough to be a man," she says.

"Mom, you don't need him. We don't need him. I've got my job and I'm gonna be the next Muhammad Ali."

"What about school?"

"I know everything I need to know." Jason arranges Cheyenne's pillows so it is easier for her to eat the soup. She starts to cough.

He hands her a tissue. "You're gonna be proud of me."

"I've always been proud of you."

"You got everything you need? I've gotta go to work." He kisses her cheek. She smiles but she is deeply worried about him. Whenever she asks Jason about the work he is doing he is evasive and dodges her questions.

Jason is committed to being the next heavyweight champion of the world. He is only 15 years old and yet he has taken on the senior patriarch role of his small family – just his mother and him. As he rides his bike down Park Ave, New York, from the Harlem end to midtown, it strikes him as totally unfair that so many people have so little and yet the few who live in the midtown Park Ave buildings have so much. His plan is to try to even out the imbalance by being an outstanding boxer and bringing to his mother the wealth that will flow from that. He has seen how she – and friends of hers - struggle through life bringing up their children to believe in strong values but too often life does not reward them for their diligence.

Jason's best friend, Keesha, has a mother who is uncaring of her which makes Jason appreciate his mother all the more. His father left when he was five years old and he hardly remembers him. As a small boy, his world was contained by the walls of his mother's apartment and the familiar Harlem streets on his walk to and from school. At his young age he has seen more than any boy should. Several of his friends are already dead and he is determined that he will not follow them. He has made compromises already in his life and has been forced into some things that he would never have chosen to do but boxing gyms need paying and he knows his mother does not have extra money for his dream. Also, since she has been sick he has shouldered the responsibility of providing the money for her medicine.

However, Jason does not believe in wasting time thinking about the unfairness of life in New York City for an African American mother and her son. He just gets on and does what needs to be done. One thing he will not do is carry a gun like so many of his friends do. Jason hates guns. He has been witness to many street fights where guns have been bought out to devastating results. His sister Analie was shot and killed as she was walking with their mother to the store for icecream. Though it was 10 years ago when Analie died at 4 years old, Jason and his mother never forget their daily ritual to send a prayer heavenwards for Analie.

FOX – USA

Several miles away from Cheyenne's apartment and her worries about Jason, Fox is walking through the forest carrying his bow and arrows. Suddenly he hears the sound of the screeching brakes of an SUV. As a Vietnam vet his army training was so comprehensive that he automatically reacts when his instincts tell him something is not quite right. At the sound of the SUV's brakes his training clicks into gear and he sprints to where the sound is coming from. He is just in time to see that the SUV has hit a deer. However, the driver does not stop. As he drives away, Fox takes an arrow out of his pack, puts it to his bow, aims and fires. The arrow lodges itself in the back left hand tire of the SUV. Satisfied, Fox bends down to examine the deer which is lying on the ground. He picks up the animal, throws it over one shoulder and walks back through the forest to his underground hideout. He lifts up the hidden trapdoor entrance and disappears down the steps.

BLACK JACK – USA

It is late evening in the back alleys of New York. The air is tense with the taste of things better not done, things better not even thought about. A police car is pulled up blocking the exit of one of those back alleys. "Black Jack" Hartnett leans on the front of his patrol car doing a line of coke. Over the course of several minutes young teenage boys walk towards him from the alley. As they get to the car Black Jack holds out his hand, into which they place various amounts of cash. He counts the cash and enters the amounts into a notebook in which he is scrupulous about his accounting. On each page a boy's name heads the page and varying dollar amounts are listed. The last boy to turn in his money is Jason. He looks nervous as Black Jack counts the cash, turning around as if he is looking for an escape route. Black Jack realizes Jason is uncomfortable. Before he has finished counting Jason's cash, he grabs his wrist. "Just hold still Flash! Let me count your cash!" He chuckles as he realizes he's made a rhyme. "Fuck! I'm as good as those asshole rappers!" He counts the last few dollars, realizing that Jason is short $100. He squeezes so tightly that Jason starts to squirm trying to get his arm free. "Where's the other benny? Don't fuck with me, Boy!"

"I'll get it, I promise. My old lady's sick. I had to get her medicine."

"I'm not buyin' that shit."

"I'll get it, I just need some time."

Black Jack begins to smile an evil grin. "Boy, today's your lucky day. Yes sir, I'm going to give you a chance to wipe the slate clean and I'll even give you some money to buy your old lady so much medicine she can stay high forever."

"She doesn't use that shit! She's sick! I told you."

"Got no insurance, eh! Well I'll give your Mamma some Black Jack Medical Insurance. And you can pay the premiums." He pulls out a gun.

TROY – USA

Troy is an integral part of his community. People care about him and he is often called in to help. He is also very willing to offer his services wherever he sees a need and his local church is one organization that seems to need him a lot.

It is annual church painting time and once again Troy is on the scene. He is helping Father O'Brien paint the interior and the pews. Well, Troy is actually doing the painting while the priest is critiquing the job. And like so many priests, Father O'Brien, over the years, has often felt he should provide fatherly advice to Troy. Though Troy is now 35, the priest still feels the need to offer his advice and give his opinions on Troy's life. Today is no exception.

"Do you think it's a good idea to teach those young boys how to fight, Troy? Aren't you just teaching them how to get into trouble?"

"No, Father. It's just the opposite. Teaching them the discipline of boxing teaches them to keep out of trouble. They learn how to handle themselves, they learn the confidence they need out on the street so they don't get pushed into things they don't really want to be a part of."

Father O'Brien is not convinced. He runs his hand over part of the wall that is not yet painted. "But the message you're giving them is that violence is acceptable."

Troy pauses with the brush in mid-air. "I don't teach them to be violent, Father. I'm showing them that they can use their intelligence at a sport - even a sport built on physical prowess - to reach a goal they often have no other means of reaching."

"Aren't you afraid they'll become bullies?"

Troy starts painting again. "Bullies are born from fear. A boy who has gained confidence in his ability as a sportsman - in whatever sport he gains that confidence - is less likely to be a bully. It's that old story, Father. Those who know their abilities and their limits don't need to cover their fears by reacting aggressively to the world at large."

"Well, I'm not entirely convinced, but I guess while they're in the boxing ring, they're not racing around the streets."

"Boxing gives them an acceptable outlet for the normal aggression that boys of that age often don't know how to handle. It gives them an idea of how to control those urges. I'm not saying that they'll never get into trouble or that boxing is going to turn little devils into choirboys but there's a discipline involved in boxing. And discipline is often something that these boys have never learnt."

SABIA – AUSTRALIA

Cottesloe Beach in West Australia is one of the world's most beautiful beaches. Sabia finds the rolling waters and the startling blueness of the waves always soothe her when she has a problem. She sneaks off as often as possible when she has something that needs thinking through. Her favourite seat on the verandah of her favourite restaurant at the beach often seems to be unoccupied and waiting for her whenever she arrives.

A soft breeze wafts over her face cooling her anxious thoughts as she watches the sun slowly sink beneath the waves of the Indian Ocean. A suntanned waitress places a cappuccino on the table in front of her. Sabia's reverie is disturbed. She smiles at the waitress. "Thanks." While waiting for her coffee Sabia has been reading a book about the culture and history of West Australia's aborigines.

The waitress, who is also Aboriginal, notices the book. "Doing some research?"

Sabia glances at the book. "Something like that."
"Oh?"

"Trying to find my birth mother. Bit belatedly though."

The waitress nods. "I know where my mother is."

Sabia is curious. "You live with her?"

"Nope. My gran's always done everything for me. Haven't seen my mother in 10 years."

"Do you miss her?"

"Hard to miss someone you don't even know."

"But you know where she is?"

"Yeah, she's hanging around some bloke who won't do her any good."

"Some women are just not very smart when it comes to men."

"Not me. I'm studying to be a lawyer. I'm not going to have some man dictating to me because he's providing an income."

"Good for you. That's what I am."

"A lawyer?"

"Almost 10 years."

"So how is it? Do you like it? Is it everything you expected?"

"You have to get used to compromise. Justice doesn't always come in a neat package."

"But at least you've got a chance to fight for justice."

"Sometimes. Just don't expect the law and justice to be synonymous."

"Had any luck finding your mother?"

"Not my birth mother. Not yet any way. Though I think I've found out where I'm from. I'm going to go and check it out."

"Are you one of the stolen ones?"

"I guess so but I'm not sure. Anyway, I wound up

with a great set of second parents."

"How do they feel about you looking for your birth mother?

"Well Dad's dead."

"I'm sorry."

"Don't be. He was very sick and I didn't want to see him suffer any more."

"And your Mum?"

"She's great. She's fine with it. She doesn't have any information though. They didn't tell her where I came from or what my real name was."

Becky, the waitress, feels for Sabia's plight. "Maybe you would like to meet my grandmother. She may be able to help you find out about your family. She's very wise – quite the tribal elder. I get off in half an hour – if you have time I could take you to meet her."

Sabia was surprised to find that she was nervous about meeting Becky's grandmother. She was worried that she wouldn't "measure up" to what might be expected of her by a woman who was wise in the ways of Aboriginal society and she was also worried that she might be judged for not trying to find her Aboriginal family earlier. However, her fears dissolved almost immediately when she met Aunty Elsie who hugged her warmly and welcomed her into her home. "Come here, daughter, let me look at you."

The short visit that Sabia was expecting extended for several hours as Aunty Elsie told her about the bad times of the stolen children. She had a wonderful sense of humor and her happy spirited attitude softened what could have been an intensely sad occasion. "You know what your name means?" she asked.

"No, does it mean something?"

"Oh yes my Sabia – your name means Daughter of the Star People. It is a very ancient name - you will find it sometimes in some of the dreamtime stories. You are blessed with your name."

It was then that Sabia pulled out her map of the Pilbara and, as she told Aunty Elsie about her visions matching the photographs in the map, the wise woman began to nod. "Then you don't need me to tell you where you are from, your spirit is talking to you."

"How?" asks Sabia.

"For thousands of years we have had a special relationship with our earth mother and everything on her – the trees, the rocks, the rivers, the lakes and waterfalls. Every animal, fish and bird is our brother or sister. Every tree is our aunty. We watch the clouds, we listen to the wind. Many, many lifetimes ago we learned to read the stars. We have so much knowledge that our spirits and our spirit people taught us in the stories of the dreamtime when the world began. For many, many lifetimes our tribal elders have passed down the knowledge of the creation stories – how the world began – in our songs and in our stories and in our dances. We pay tribute to our animal brothers and sisters in our dances and songs because they give up their lives for us. Not their spirit lives but their earthly lives. Their spirit lives go on – just like ours do."

Sabia is enthralled. "Why doesn't European society take more notice of your history and culture?" she asks.

Aunty Elsie sighs. "Fear."

"Fear?" queries Sabia.

"Pure and simple fear," says Aunty Elsie, "fear comes from ignorance. Way back then they were afraid we would claim what was ours. And they wanted what was ours. So they tried to pretend that we didn't exist. They did many bad things to try to wipe us out, but we survived. They failed. So then they decided to steal our future by taking our children and trying to turn them into white children."

Sabia is unsettled. She feels that she has been party to something dishonest.

Aunty Elsie pats her hand. "Don't take it so hard, child. None of this is your fault. This is what happens when two worlds collide. One side will always be stronger and, too often, the leaders of the strongest are not the wisest leaders but simply the more fearful."

TROY – USA

On the other side of the world Troy is in the gym with Jason. He's pacing Jason who is pummeling away at the punching bag. Troy gives him the timing for his punches. "Hit! Hit! Hit! Hit! Hit! Hit!" Jason punches the bag in time to the rhythm of Troy's speech. Troy speeds up the rhythm and Jason speeds up his fists. The boy shows talent but Troy can see that he is not as focused as he normally is. After the session, as they walk up the basement stairs, Troy tackles Jason. "Is anything wrong, Jason?"

"Nothing I can't sort out."

"Do you want to talk about it?"

"I can handle it."

Later as Troy walks with Tiger through the night-time streets he is thinking about Jason and wondering what it is that is taking his attention away from boxing. As he walks past the corner bodega owned by his neighbor and friend, Mrs Lopez, she sees him through the shop window. Waving him into the shop she pours him a cup of coffee. Troy tries to pay for the coffee but Mrs Lopez waves away his money. "Friends don't pay for coffee," she smiles at him. "And how is my favorite dog, Tiger," she says as she stoops down to rub Tiger's golden coat. Mrs Lopez and her bodega often serve as the local community center where neighbors drop in to talk, catch up on the local street news and gossip, share a coffee and buy their ticket to Lotto fortune and the fulfillment of their dreams. Many New York neighborhoods where people would gather on their front stoops to escape the heat of the long, hot summer streets and to exchange gossip with their neighbors were dislocated as the brownstones were bulldozed to accommodate freeways. So corner stores – bodegas – have to some extent taken the place of the streetside gathering centers. Of course they are not always run by such cheery souls as Mrs Lopez with some serving as fronts for drug dealers. Mrs Lopez has a soft spot for Troy. Not having her own children she looks to Troy as the son she would have had if she had been fortunate enough to be blessed with one. Though Troy is appreciative of Mrs Lopez' attitude towards him, he has always been guarded in his friendships.

After he leaves the bodega Troy walks back home still thinking about Jason and wondering how he can help the teen. As if his thoughts materialize before his eyes Jason appears out of an alley two blocks further on from where Troy is walking. Jason shoots out of the alley on his bike as if a ghost is chasing him. Troy calls out to Jason but he rides off in the other direction. As Troy looks after Jason a police car creeps out of the alley and drives past Troy, the driver not noticing him but Troy notices the driver. It is Black Jack. He knows the neighborhood gossip about him and it is all bad.

SABIA – AUSTRALIA

After her visit with Aunty Elsie, Sabia has decided to follow her instincts and she is now barrelling along Great Northern Highway driving back into the past to retrace her origins. A truck comes swooping down the highway going in the other direction. The driver waves at her and she waves back. She has been on the road for hours and notices that her fuel is low. She pulls in to a service station. A man comes out to fill up her car.

"What's your poison, Luv?"

"Super. Fill it up, please."

"Goin' far?"

"A fair way."

"Bet you're goin' home."

"Something like that."

"Ya folks must miss you."

"Yeah."

"Watch out for roos when you're drivin'."

"Are they a problem?"

"Too right. Specially at sundown. That's when they come out to cross the road. They're hard to see. If one of them big buggers comes through your windscreen, you'll be totally cactus."

"Thanks. I'll keep an eye out."

"No worries, Luv. And make sure you keep your tank full. Could be a strike comin' up soon."

"A fuel strike?"

"Transport strike. They're goin' for a pay rise. They'll pull a strike as sure as eggs is eggs and that'll tie up fuel for weeks."

"How do you know?"

"I may be a hundred miles from nowhere, but I always know what's goin' on. I've been ordering extra fuel for the past few weeks, I don't want to get caught short."

"How bad will it be?"

"No deliveries and no planes flyin' for a while."

"Thanks. I'll remember."

"Be seein' ya, Luv. Safe trip."

Sabia gets back on the highway thinking about what the gas guy said. She makes a mental note to pull in and fill up every time she gets to a service station.

As the day's shadows lengthen, the kangaroos are stirring. Sabia sees them bounding across the paddock next to the road. She is wary even though it is beautiful countryside. As far as she can see on both sides of the road are what appear to be carpets of colour. It is wildflower season and thousands of wildflowers line the road and spread across the horizon. She realizes as she looks across the multi-coloured paddocks that she has never been this far out of the city before and she berates herself for missing out on such spectacular scenery all her life. Maybe it is childhood memories that have held her back. She feels something stirring inside her like a memory she can't quite remember.

Unknown to Sabia it is exactly this time of the year when she and Troy were taken from their mother thirty years ago and, not very many miles from where she is driving, Rose is back in her familiar bush camp. Tidying her camp, she stops and looks up at the sky. Her deep Aboriginal instincts alert her to something. She can feel deep inside her heart that someone is coming. For thirty years, no matter where life has taken her, Rose has always returned to the bush camp on the anniversary of the taking of Troy and Sabia. She tells herself every year: "Maybe this year they will come." It is this strong belief that has made it possible for her to put one foot in front of the other and keep going. It is this strong belief that has let her continue to take one breath after another when all her heart wanted her to do was shut down and close her eyes never to open them again. Rose is beginning to feel that her long wait is almost over. She adds another log to the fire to provide a warming welcome.

A lonely bird wings lazily above the highway turnoff where Sabia has paused in her journey. She has had to make an urgent toilet stop and, squatting down behind some roadside bushes, she notices the bird. Some chord seems to flutter in her chest and she begins to feel that this place is familiar. Getting back in the car she makes the decision to turn off the highway and explore this side road. Is this the road back to her past as a girl living free in the bush? As she drives past a pyramid-shaped hill, she is becoming more certain that this is where she belongs. A lone emu runs along beside the car keeping pace with her and sometimes getting ahead of her. She shakes her head and smiles. "Fancy being outrun by a bird."

It is a hot, still afternoon so Sabia parks her car under the shade of a gumtree. She gets out and stands on top of a cliff overlooking the river. The red of the iron ore cliff strikes a sharp contrast with the olive green of the trees along the riverbank. Putting her arms out as if she can fly, a feeling of peace envelopes her as the wind gently stirs her hair.

In an echo of her previous daydream, cockatoos float effortlessly on the air currents above the river. Slowly they turn and settle on the tree branches beginning their daily drink. Sabia's stomach starts to alert her to the familiarity of this place. She is becoming more aware that this is the place of her childhood but it seems deserted. How will she ever find anyone who can tell her anything about her early life? But on this day, she will not have to go far to find her confirmation. From the other side of the river Rose watches Sabia unseen as she gets back in her car and starts to drive away from the river. There is a small road bridge over which she is driving slowly. Underneath is a huge pipe diverting some of the water from the river. A wall has been built around one side of it creating a natural spa. Sabia is hot. She stops the car, gets out. There is no-one around. She quickly strips off her clothes and wades into the water. She is enjoying the bubbles when suddenly about ten Aboriginal kids appear out of the bush - as if by magic. Giggling and laughing they jump in the water right next to her, almost drowning her. They splash her and play with her, not at all surprised that she has suddenly appeared in their favourite swimming hole. Though she is slightly embarrassed about being naked, they are not. The squeals of delight of the children keep her attention on the water. If she only chose to look up maybe she would see that behind a large gumtree at the edge of the pool Rose is watching her.

The children suddenly splash their way out of the pool and disappear into the bush as if obeying some invisible command. Sabia is now alone. Trying to hide her nakedness she quickly dresses and gets back in her car. Driving slowly, she sees the turnoff to Python Pool. She drives slowly down the track, parks the car and walks down to the pool. The blood red cliffs fall jaggedly down to the emerald green water. This time she is taking no chances. She changes into a swimsuit. At the edge of the pool she looks up to the red, high cliffs. The sun is in her eyes. She squints them shut. Cupping her hands she scoops up some water, takes it in her mouth and blows it up into the air. The sun splits the water droplets and a perfect miniature rainbow is held for a moment in the air above the pool. Sabia slides silently into the cool green waters. What the sun has stopped her from seeing is a snake, which slithers down from the hot red cliffs. It is ready for a drink. It enters the water noiselessly, leaving a slight trail in the water.

From her hiding place at the top of the cliffs Rose sees the snake. She calls out to Sabia but she doesn't hear as her head is under the water and a bunch of white cockatoos are screeching in the trees above the pool.

"Snake!" yells Rose. "Look out!" But Sabia is oblivious of the danger. She swims as if she were part of the pool and the rocks. She is at one with this outback place. She can feel the muscles in her stomach relax and she feels that she is home.

Suddenly and swiftly the snake strikes! Sabia recoils in shock. She sees the form as the snake swims away. Has she transgressed some ancient custom? Was she trespassing on sacred ground? But no time to think about that. She must get help. She is not aware of Rose but Rose is only too aware of what is happening to Sabia. The cliffs are a sheer drop down and the water is shallow. Rose knows she can't dive into the pool. The only way to Sabia is to go around the edge of the pool to the small track which leads to the water. These will be precious minutes when the snake's poison will be coursing through her bloodstream. Precious minutes that could figure in saving her life. Rose is distressed almost to breaking point as she races through the bush to get to Sabia.

Sabia is shocked and, struggling out of the water, she holds her arm. Though she thinks she is alone, she cries out for help. "Help me! Someone! I've been bitten." Just then Rose comes running down the track. Sabia is surprised to see anyone here but she is intensely grateful that she is not alone. "I've been bitten by a snake. I need a doctor."

"Doctors are too far away. No time for that."

"But I've been bitten by a snake."

"I'm here." Quickly Rose helps Sabia sit against a tree trunk in the shade. She tears the bottom of her skirt and wraps it around Sabia's arm. Finishing the bandaging she places a wet towel on her head. "The bandage will stop the poison flowing while I make your medicine."

Rose quickly fills a pot with water and places it over the fire, then collects leaves from several of the trees and shrubs around the pool adding the leaves to the pot. Soon Rose pours some of the liquid from the pot into a coffee mug, holding Sabia's head as she sips. "Drink slowly, daughter. It's hot. This will cure you." Sabia sips from the mug.

Rose re-wets the towel and gently wipes the sweat from Sabia's face. In between sips of the healing tea, she gives her sips of cool water to carry the healing herbs throughout her body to fight the snake's venom.

Sunset sends brilliant colourful streaks across the scattered clouds as Rose continues her vigil. Dusk brings a cool breeze which blows softly over the two women. Sleep will now bring the final healing to Sabia as Rose slides a small pillow behind her head. She knows Sabia would be more comfortable if she helped her lie down on Rose's small airbed but she does not want to move her and perhaps aggravate the snake's venom through her system. Quiet and calmness is needed for Sabia's cure.

"Sleep now little one. We will talk more tomorrow. Get your rest."

While Sabia sleeps, Rose keeps a watchful eye on her long-lost daughter. She mops her face as Sabia sweats out the snake's poison. Several times during the night Rose offers Sabia cool water to drink which Sabia sips half-asleep. As she watches over her, Rose is relieved and amazed that after all this time she finally has her daughter – now a beautiful young woman – in front of her. How many times had she imagined this meeting? How many times had she played it through her mind worrying that she would die before she saw her two beloved children again. She long ago gave up the bitterness she had felt when they were taken from her that desperate night. And then she remembers the dream she had of Troy the night before. The details are now quite hazy but she remembers the black snake that had coiled itself around Troy, though in her dream he was still a young boy, not a grown man which he must be by now. In her dream the snake was swimming in the ocean and Rose's instincts tell her that Troy is overseas.

As dawn begins to sneak its feathery fingers across the Pilbara sky, Rose finally begins to relax. She knows that Sabia has beaten the snake and she will wake gently soon. She sets her fishing lines in the pool waiting for her to wake up. The north west sun is hot even in the early morning. It wakes Sabia who shades her eyes. Rose is right. Sabia has recovered from the snakebite. Sabia rubs the two puncture wounds on her arm and then smiles at Rose who hands her a cup of coffee.

"You are better. The snake's poison has left you."

While Sabia finishes her coffee Rose pulls out two fish which are snagged on her lines. She cleans and fries them over the campfire for breakfast.

As they eat the fish Rose feels that she can now tell Sabia who she is. "It's been many years, daughter. I knew you would come."

Sabia suddenly realizes what Rose is saying. "You've mistaken me for someone else. I've only just arrived."

But Rose is sure. "No. This is where you were born. This is your sit-down country. My baby! They took you away, my Sabia, my star daughter. And now you are back home."

Sabia thinks maybe she is daydreaming or delirious from the snake's poison. How does this woman know her name? "You know my name? You are my mother?"

A single tear rolls down Rose's cheek. "You are my daughter Sabia."

Sabia is overcome. She can't speak. Her tears flow freely. If this really is her mother, she may be Sabia's salvation.

Rose nods her head. "I knew you would come."

"How did you know?"

"I sent you a thought message."

"You sent me a thought message?" says Sabia. "After all this time? Why now? Why not before?"

"For thirty years I have come here every year waiting for you. The time is urgent now because I want to see my children again before I die."

"I have sisters...and brothers?"

"Your brother Troy."

"Troy? Where is he?"

"I dreamt about him the other night."

"How can I find him?"

"There will be news."

"News?" Sabia is puzzled.

"Watch for the news."

"You come here every year?" asks Sabia trying to find a lead in to what she really wants to know.

Rose tells her that she visits this camp on the anniversary of their taking every year.

"But why didn't you send me a thought message before?" Sabia is anxious to know.

"I didn't want to interfere with your life. I knew that many of our babies were given to white families. I thought if you grew up in a white family and I suddenly appeared it may upset you. I wanted you to find me yourselves when you were ready but now it has become urgent. I have not much time left."

Sabia is ever the pragmatist. "But what do the doctors say?"

"I don't need doctors to tell me what I already know." Rose pours Sabia another cup of coffee. "Now that you're better I want to show you something."

The sun shines down brightly on them as if the sky is celebrating the return of Sabia. As they walk through the bush to the lilypond they are watched by two kangaroos. The kangaroos are still as the two women walk by and soon reach the palmtree-shaded lilypond.

Rose holds Sabia's hand as she leads her out into the water in the middle of the lilypond. On one of the waterlily leaves is a small, bright green frog. Rose gently picks up the frog and puts it on the palm of her left hand. She begins to stroke the frog down its back and, as she strokes, the frog begins to sing - well - croak. Rose talks very softly so as not to disturb the frog. "My totem is the frog. This is one of my brothers. You hear him sing? I can send a message out through my frog brothers. He sings to his friends and they sing the message to their friends and so it goes on and on and on like a ripple on a pond."

Sabia is intrigued. "Totem? Do I have a totem?" Rose places the frog gently back on the waterlily leaf.

"Kangaroo. You and your brother are of the skin of the kangaroo."

Sabia looks at the skin on her arm. "Pity it wasn't the skin of the snake."

Rose ignores her joke. "The skin of the kangaroo is strong, like you..... and Troy."

"Not strong enough to stop them from taking us from you."

Rose touches her long-lost daughter lightly on the face. "People make a mistake with the kangaroo. They think he is soft and furry. True, he is not easily riled to anger but he's very dangerous if cornered."

"Dangerous?"

"A kangaroo can disembowel a man in three seconds."

"How?"

"He leans back on his strong tail and rips with his back feet. Those claws are sharp."

"Mum......," Sabia hesitates, it seems strange calling another woman 'Mum'. Rose understands. "You can call me Rose."

"Rose, what happened to you after they took us away?"

"I ran after you as far as I could until I was so exhausted I collapsed on the ground. As soon as I did, another car pulled up. They'd come to get me too."

"Why didn't they keep us together?"

"Their ways are strange."

"Where did they take you?"

"They put me in a mission place at first but every chance I would get I would run away trying to find you and Troy."

"Then what happened?"

"They'd come after me each time and take me back. I'd wait my chance and escape again."

"Good on you."

"After so many escapes the mission people handed me over to the police sargeant."

"The police?"

"He was a hard man. Thought he could stop me."

Sadness sweeps over Sabia who is beginning to understand how much she and Troy meant to their mother, their Aboriginal mother.

"He tried to starve me and let me die of thirst."

Sabia is shocked about what Rose has been through. "What did he do to you?"

Rose's eyes seem to mist over as she recalls the days and nights and the hardships she has seen. "He loaded me into the back of his ute (pick up truck) and handcuffed me so I couldn't jump out. It was hot, so hot. I like the sun but even for me that was too hot. For hours and hours we travelled on dirt and dusty roads. He took backtracks so no-one would see how he was treating me. I think he was trying to kill me on that trip."

Sabia can't believe any woman could be treated so badly. "That's terrible." She reaches over and holds Rose's hand.

Rose smiles at the thought of her plan. "I was planning to play possum when he finally stopped, but I didn't have to. I was so exhausted I had fainted in the back of that hot, hot ute. So he had to lift me out himself. He thought I was dead." Sabia's eyes are full of tears. "What did he do then?"

"He panicked in case anyone asked questions about me - people at the mission or his bosses back at the station. So he finally had to give me some water."

"Where had he taken you?"

"Up north."

"Where?"

"To the jail in the tree."

Sabia is puzzled. "A jail in a tree?"

Rose nods. "It's a boab tree – very, very, very old tree – a thousand years or more. They used to use it as a jail and the sargeant decided that's where he would put me. "

Sabia is astounded. "So he locked you up inside a tree? For how long? I mean he let you out again? He was just trying to frighten you, wasn't he?"

"He left me there for two weeks. No food, no water. He really did want me to die but some of these white fellers are just pug ignorant about us."

Sabia is silently weeping. Rose pats her hand. "Don't cry, my Sabia. You can see I'm here. He didn't kill me, that sargeant. I'm stronger than him."

"What did you do? How did you get food… and water?"

Rose smiles a wide grin. "My sister tree, she fed me and gave me water."

Sabia doesn't understand. "The tree gave you food and water?"

Rose chuckles. "Best bush tucker, that tree." She holds up her hands signifying a large nut. "Big nuts, she has, my sister tree. Big like this and sweet, ooh delicious." She smacks her lips. "And all my sister and brother honey ants, they visited me every day, bringing me their honey. Nice and sweet, those ants."

"But what about water?"

Rose grins again. "I drank my sister tree's tears."

Sabia doesn't understand. "You drank her tears?"

"Yes," Rose nods. "Sister tree has big juicy roots. Every night she sucks up water and in the morning, her tears slide down the inside of her trunk to water the tree. I drank the tears of my sister tree."

At last Sabia is beginning to understand the true strength of the spirit of her long ago mother, Rose. "How did you get away from the sargeant?"

Rose smiles again. "I made him fed up with me."

"What do you mean?" asks Sabia.

"When he sees that I am not dead, that I am living and well even though he starves me and gives me no water, he just gets fed up with me. One day he comes, says nothing, unlocks the door and walks away. No more sargeant. I am free."

"What happened then?"

"I tried to find you and Troy. I travelled around anywhere where there were piccinniny kids. I got some jobs working on stations as a cook but every year at the same time - the time they took you away - I would come back to the pool and camp here for a few weeks. Waiting."

"Waiting?"

"Waiting for you and Troy to come back. And finally you have."

"You've come back here every year for thirty years?" Sabia hugs her mother - such devotion. She feels that the time is right for her to ask Rose if she will come down to Perth and have the tests as her possible donor but she is worried about Rose's health so she hesitates. Suddenly Rose's breathing becomes labored. Her head starts to sink and she looks as if she will faint.

"Rose, what is it?" asks Sabia, very worried.

"Here, lean on me." She takes Rose by the arms and helps her out of the lilypond gently laying her under the shade of a palm tree. "Is it the heat? Are you thirsty?" She undoes her water bottle and offers it to Rose.

"Please don't worry, my daughter. I will be fine. It is just sometimes I have trouble getting my breath. It will go in a minute."

After Rose has rested, Sabia helps her back to the camp. She spends a worried night watching over her and decides she cannot ask Rose to be tested as her donor but she does want to take her to a medical center.

The next morning a brilliant sunrise lights the sky as Sabia prepares to leave. She puts her bag in the car, then turns to Rose who hands her a small bag. Sabia opens the bag and sees that it contains earth. "What's this?"

Rose places her hand over Sabia's as she holds the bag of earth. "This is the earth of your country. Take it to remind you of where you belong."

Sabia is touched. "I want you to come with me so I can take you to a doctor. I want them to check out your breathing."

"Doctors can't help me. My time is almost here, but my daughter, I know you are sick. I will come. They need to test me don't they?"

"I didn't want to ask you when you are sick yourself," says Sabia feeling guilty about possibly putting Rose through another ordeal. Rose touches Sabia's face. "I am your mother. My blood is your blood." Rose brings out a bag that she had already packed. She puts it in the car and gets in. Sabia and Rose drive down the same road the men drove down when they took the children away thirty years ago.

BLACK JACK - USA

Two oceans away, a very different sargeant of police is getting ready to leave his apartment. It is late in the Strong household. Sargeant Strong tries to allay the fears of his wife, Delores, as he puts his gun in his underarm holster. She is worried. "Be careful. I don't trust him."

Squeezing her shoulder he says: "Don't worry, Del. It'll be all right."

But she is not convinced. "I think you're making a big mistake. Black Jack didn't get that name because he's a pussycat. He's bad through and through."

"I'm not going to tell them anything."

"It's Internal Affairs. You can't just refuse to answer their questions."

"They can't force me."

"Please be careful. Black Jack will try to stop you from talking to them."

"I've told you. It'll be fine. I'm just meeting with him to go over my answers for internal affairs. Now give me a kiss and stop worrying."

Strong is not under any illusions about his meeting with Black Jack. He knows he might never see Del again after tonight. Black Jack is a dangerous enemy but he is also a dangerous friend and, as his police partner, the sargeant has walked a slippery tightrope. Trying to stay on the straight and narrow is very hard for a cop with a crooked partner. Strong knows that Black Jack has many friends in the criminal world – people he has done favors for over the years, from evidence that mysteriously disappears, to notification of raids on criminal premises to drug deals that have seen Black Jack getting progressively richer. Not to say that Black Jack hasn't been smart.

He has hidden the cash in small construction projects on his house always making sure to get a personal loan from his bank to seemingly provide the money for each project that then allowed him to mix in some of the illegal money he had received. But Black Jack's luck has run out and internal affairs have finally decided to shine their spotlight on him.

Sargeant Strong knows that tonight could be his last night. He has been rehearsing his upcoming conversation with Black Jack but he also knows that the pressure he will be under from the internal affairs interrogators will be intense – as Black Jack knows too. One of the interrogators in particular has Black Jack in his sights.

Strong is sweating as he slides into the driver's seat of his patrol car. He feels that driving the police car to the meet with Black Jack might somehow protect him rather than driving his own anonymous car. He knows this particular block of Brooklyn well as he often calls in for a coffee at Mrs Lopez's bodega and he always makes a joke with her about his lotto winnings – which have so far amounted to a measly $1200 but she always promises him the winning ticket "for sure this time."

As Black Jack drives to the meet with Strong he is feeling elated. Tonight – in a few minutes – most of his worries will be over. The one person who knows more about his deals than anyone else will be dead and Black Jack won't have had to do it himself. That stupid punk kid will take the rap and Black Jack will have shot him as soon as he is finished shooting Strong. That will tie everything up nicely. There will be no surprises, he assures himself. All he was doing was stopping his partner's killer from getting away. Perfectly natural response on his part. There will be an inquiry, as there always is, but with no witnesses who could doubt his story. Black Jack is expecting Jason to run towards him after he shoots Strong so he has worked out exactly where he should be when Jason fires.

At the same time and just a few blocks from where Black Jack parks his car to meet with Strong, Troy is putting on Tiger's leash to take him for a late night walk. He comes out of his apartment with Tiger. The streets are deserted as they walk.

Meanwhile at an alley just a few streets away Black Jack holds a gun to Jason's head. "He'll be here soon. You'll do it and if you fuck this up I'll rape your mother."

Strong drives down the street and stops at the corner. On the opposite corner Black Jack waves to him. He signals to Strong to wait while he crosses the street. Strong gets out of his car and stands on the sidewalk to wait for Black Jack to cross.

From behind a parked car two car lengths away from where Strong has pulled up, Jason appears. He runs up to the sargeant, points the gun and shoots him in the neck, not stopping to take aim. The bullet slices Strong's jugular vein. Blood spurts all over Jason. He takes off running back the way he came, not looking where he is going as Black Jack reaches Strong.

Troy hears the shot. Tiger takes fright, yanks against the lead and races off down the street. As Troy is about to go after him, Jason comes racing round the corner. He runs straight into Troy almost knocking him over. As he does so he smears blood on Troy's shirt and pushes the gun into Troy's hand. Then he's gone. In the few seconds that he saw him, Troy realizes that it is Jason. That's all he has time to register before he is grabbed by Black Jack who comes running around the corner. "Boy, you're dead! I'm gonna fill you full of lead like you did Strong!" Then Black Jack realizes that it is not Jason but a man who is smeared with blood and holding a gun. Taken off balance he smashes his gun into Troy's face. Troy slumps to the ground, out cold.

"What the fuck," says Black Jack. "Where's that Motherfucker?" Black Jack is in a quandary. He wants to go after Jason so he can kill him but what to do about this blood-smeared man with the gun. He immediately recognized the gun Troy is holding because he had given Jason a gun he had stolen from a crime scene several years ago. It has a distinctive butt and, as a collector of guns, Black Jack just could not resist taking it for his collection. Instantly he makes his decision. Put a bullet into the man lying at his feet and then go after Jason and finish him off but he must call in the shooting first.

Unbeknown to Black Jack however, Mrs Lopez has heard a shot and has called 911. Just as Black Jack aims at Troy two uniformed police reach him stopping him from shooting. "This the perp?"

"This motherfucker killed my partner." Black Jack has made his decision.

The uniforms take over. They think Troy's dead because of the blood. They can see that Black Jack is upset and angry. They think it is because his partner's been shot and killed but Black Jack is worrying about how he is going to clean up this mess. Furious at Jason for deviating from his plan by running back the way he had come instead of straight to where Black Jack was going to be, he knows he will have to track down Jason and kill him. And he'll have to call in some favors to have Troy found guilty of Strong's death. "He's out cold, not dead," says Black Jack.

"You didn't kill this motherfucker?" one of the cops asks Black Jack, puzzled. But Black Jack doesn't hear as he walks back to where Strong lies on the street.

News travels fast and bad news travels at the speed of light. There is a football scrum waiting outside the court building as Troy is pushed out of the door by the cops into the glare of the publicity machine. There are shouts of "cop killer" from some of the crowd which has gathered as he is pushed into a police van and driven away. Some of the TV camerapeople run down the street trying to get that last elusive, exclusive shot. Finally giving up, a cameraman shuts down his equipment. "He's just walking dead."

JASON – USA

Meanwhile, Jason is just getting back to his mother's apartment. He has been hiding in back alleys and he spent several hours in a street bin trying to work out what he should do. As he raced past a barbershop window the TV news showed Sargeant Strong's death and Troy being taken in as the killer. Jason knows that even though Troy has been blamed for the killing, while Jason is still alive he is a distinct threat to Black Jack. No matter what happens to Troy, Jason knows that Black Jack will kill him. He knows too that that must have been Black Jack's plan all along. The uncanny co-incidence that saw Troy at the wrong place at the wrong time will not change Black Jack's determination to kill Jason, he knows. He is not sure where he will go but he knows that it is far too dangerous for him to stay here even though he feels that he is deserting his mother at her time of need. Jason tries to be as quiet as possible as he comes through the front door of Cheyenne's apartment. In the gloom Cheyenne can't see him.

"Jason, is that you? Where've you been? I've been so worried about you."

"Mom, I'm going to be away for a few days. Keesha will look after you while I'm gone." Cheyenne's alarm shows in her voice. "Where are you going? Jason. What's wrong?"

"Don't worry Mom. Everything will be all right. I promise. Just tell Keesha anytime you need something. She'll stay with you." Jason gives his mother a kiss and then quietly slips back out the door.

TROY – USA

Prisons are no place anyone should ever be if they have no reason to be there and Troy knew that he was going to have to practice all his mental skills if he was going to last or at least survive this experience. He had already given up hope of the truth being known. He knew he could never give up Jason to save himself. Troy knows what will be in store for him.

As a 'cop killer' the guards will look for any possible situation they can to punish him. Not just punish him as they would any inmate but he will be singled out for special treatment. The agenda will be to make his life miserable. There will not be a second when he will not have to be on his guard. For Troy this experience will be akin to the time he spent during the war in Vietnam. There was no knowing who the enemy was.

The toll of being on guard every minute of every day was something he had schooled into himself. Some men couldn't take it. Others let their guard down, to their cost. Troy had never forgotten the lessons he had learned in that faraway country and he mentally put himself back there again as he focused on a talisman to direct his attention away from the pain he knew he was about to endure.

Troy withdrew into an inner world where no-one else could go. He thought of Tiger, his beloved dog. Tiger was going to be his focus for however long he would be locked up and for whatever the outcome of this stage of his life. Like war, prison is something that he will endure.

That first night was a brutal welcome. He was stark naked. A guard stood with a leer on his face and a hose in his hand. They were in the shower area and Troy should have been showering himself but that is a luxury he was not to be afforded that night. A second guard reached for the cold water tap turning it right around to full on. "Freeze that cocksucker's balls off." BAM! The freezing water hit Troy like a freight train at full speed. Troy was almost knocked over but he stood his ground.

MATHIAS – USA

Unknown to Troy at the same time as he is being introduced to prison life, across town in a seedy basement billiard parlor someone else is trying to survive the vicissitudes of the legal profession. But where Troy is determined not to give up hope that he will one day progress past his current circumstances, Mathias Swinebourne long ago gave up any hope he may have once felt. Feelings are not something that Mathias has contemplated in a very long time. He has a chip on his shoulder the size of an Egyptian pyramid. Life hasn't knocked it off so far, so it's probably set in stone. He doesn't care about anyone or anything. The one bright hope in his life walked out, making hamburger meat of his heart and hamburger meat of his wallet. If he could get up the energy or the passion he would probably end his life, but even that seems like too much trouble, so he's stuck in a life he doesn't want, going through the motions of being a successful lawyer. He's not stupid, don't think that, but he's spent a life in the shadow of his older brother Matthew. "Matthew the Wonder Dog" Mathias always calls him with a shard of sarcasm in his voice. Some people misunderstand and think he is expressing his respect for his older brother, who ironically is also a lawyer - another barb in Mathias' back. Quelle domage! A brilliant man suffering a life of self-strangulation and too damned apathetic to care. Nothing and no-one will ever convince him to feel any other way. We meet Mathias in a particularly black mood. Today's hangover would have needed dynamite to persuade it to shift. Today's booze has only made it worse. It is 3am and to avoid the prospect of going to bed, Mathias is playing billiards by himself. Smack! He hits the red. It heads straight for the pocket. Just before it disappears down the velvet hole, a hand appears - like the disconnected hand of God - and plucks it off the table. Mathias is furious. "What the fuck!" The hand belongs to Black Jack. His ferocious face leers at Mathias with his other hand resting quietly on his holstered pistol.

Mathias' eyes blaze red. "Whatdyathink you're doing, asshole?"

Black Jack leans across the table. "Don't tempt me."

"Put it back!" shouts Mathias.

Black Jack throws the red across the room. "Listen up, Sunshine. I've got a proposition for you." He pulls out his gun and places it on the billiard table.

Mathias fingers the billiard cube, debating whether he should smack Black Jack across the head with it. "What the fuck could you possibly have to tell me that I'd be interested in hearing?"

Black Jack hears the note of interest in Mathias' voice. "One word. Money. The language that everybody speaks. Money."

Mathias lines up another ball turning away from Black Jack. "I don't want your fuckin' money."

Black Jack reaches into his pocket and pulls out a thick wad of gambling IOUs. "You may not want it, but Sunshine, you need it." He waves the IOUs at Mathias in a taunting dance. "Lady Luck has kissed your ass goodbye and the Man was getting impatient."

Mathias makes a low growl and spits on the table. "You know what you can do with those Sunshine! You can shove them right up where the sun don't shine!"

TROY – USA

Troy has survived his first few hours in prison by completely withdrawing into himself. He hasn't spoken to anyone. He didn't complain or resist the ice-cold shower treatment by the guards. He has decided that staying silent is the best way he can continue to survive what he knows is in store for him. He gets his meal, finds the most isolated spot in the prison dining room and sits down.

Three prison guards are in a huddle in one corner of the room. "That motherfucker's gonna wish he had never come through the door," says one as the others grunt in agreement.

Troy tries a mouthful of his food but his stomach nerves are in such a knot that he pushes his tray away just as the First Guard reaches him.

"Food's not up to your standard eh, you fucking scum. Let me improve it for you." He tips the tray of food on the floor. Then squashes one of his boots in it. "Come on Big Killer Man. Let's see you eat this."

Troy doesn't move. The guard loses his temper. He grabs Troy, shoving him to the floor near the food. "I said: Eat it." Troy remains totally rigid, not even a hair on his head moves. The guard pulls out his gun and cocks it against Troy's right ear. "I said: Eat it."

Just then Warden Django walks through the door. He takes in the disturbance at a glance. "On your feet, Washington." He gestures to the guard. "Put your gun away. Have this mess cleaned up."

Later that night Troy sits on his bunk thinking about his future and what the possibilities are for him. At least he has the cell to himself. Isolated from his familiar life he realizes that, in all probability, he will not survive. He will be a target inside the prison and if he survives that, the law will probably legally kill him for his role as a 'cop killer'. He knows he cannot give up Jason so any defense argument in court is closed to him. He is not a quitter but in the depths of his soul he feels that this is one time that he has no real control over his life. He has not had the kind of life that he had hoped for but he feels he has made a contribution in his own small way but he cannot see any way out of his present predicament. The one thing Troy is determined about is that he will not allow himself to be killed. If he is to die it will be by his own hand and in his own time. Until that time he will remain on guard. Determined to keep his focus strong, his thoughts become of Tiger who has been his constant companion since his parents died. He is worried about Tiger and plans to ask for the chance to ring Mrs Lopez to see if she has seen him anywhere. Troy feels sure that Tiger would have found his way back home and hopes he is waiting on the steps expecting Troy to return home.

The next day Troy is surprised to be taken to the visitors' room where Mrs Lopez is waiting for him.

"Hello son." Troy is puzzled. Mrs Lopez is not his mother. She puts her fingers to his lips to shush him in case the guard hears. "They said only your mother or your closest blood relatives could visit," whispers Mrs Lopez. "What can I do for you? Do you need anything?"

"Find Tiger and look after him please."

"Don't worry, he's home with me right now. I'll look after him until this is sorted out and you're home again."

"That may be a very long time, if ever," says Troy. He is immensely relieved to be told by Mrs Lopez that she found Tiger scratching at her back door when she closed up the shop last night. It was then that she saw the midnight news report of his arrest. "I know you didn't do it. They'll work it out eventually. Just wait, you'll see." She looks at the door. "Poor Tiger. I see him looking at the door every minute waiting for you to come walking through it."

"There's something else I need you to do, please."

"Anything, Troy. Just ask."

"I've been visiting kids in hospital – kids who need special care. I need you to visit Suzy and explain to her that I won't be able to get to see her for some time but that I am thinking of her and I am still her friend."

Mrs Lopez is happy to be able to do something to help Troy. She asks for more information about Suzy and she is shocked at what Troy tells her. She says she will visit Suzy as soon as she leaves and let her know that Troy is thinking of her.

MATHIAS – USA

The next night, Mathias is passing through the prison receiving area. He has decided to visit one of his clients early in the evening so he will have a clear run at boozing and gambling later on. As he's being let in through the gate he pats his pockets as if he is looking for something. He is shown down the corridor by the guard on duty. "Someone wants to see you before you go in," says the guard. Mathias ignores him as they walk through to the next gated section. Two other guards watch as they walk past.

"Who's the poor sucker who's got him as his lawyer?" one of the guards asks the other guard who has only just joined the prison team.

"Whadya mean?"

"Swinebourne. His wife got a big divorce settlement. And he plays the ponies. Word is he's always after the Benjamins. Whoever's got the most money will get the verdict they want - he'll do everything short of bribing the judge to get the right verdict."

"What about appeals?"

"He's not stupid. He always makes a good case. He just knows how not to make it a great case."

The escort guard stands back as Mathias enters

the office, shuts the door and waits outside. Black Jack has been waiting inside the office.

Mathias sees Black Jack. He's not happy. "You again. Whaddya want?"

Black Jack ignores the question. "How much do you owe your ex, Matthew?"

"Mathias, Motherfucker."

"So how much paper do you need?"

Mathias is getting angry now. "Look you fucker. What are you wasting my time for? I told you what you could do."

Black Jack is not to be denied. "You're already here. You might as well go and see him. Convince him to plead guilty. Half a day in court - come back in a few weeks for the sentencing - you're gone. And your ex is off your back."

"Fuck you."

Black Jack's face looks like thunder. "You're no virgin." He hands Mathias an envelope. "Do yourself a favor. Keep her sweet. Just make sure your boy pleads guilty. Do your job."

Mathias looks at the envelope. "Like you're doing your job."

Black Jack's eyes take on a blacker hue. "Don't fuck with me. Don't ever fuck with me."

Mathias feels the wad of money inside the envelope. It would get a lot of pressure off. He pockets the envelope.

A few minutes later Mathias is shown into Troy's cell.

"Who are you?" asks Troy.

"Mathias Swinebourne. I'm your lawyer."

"I can't afford a lawyer."

"Don't worry. You don't have to pay. I'm doing this out of the goodness of my heart."

"Yeah, and I still believe in Santa Claus." Mathias sneers at Troy. "And I'm very happy for you."

"So what's this all about?" asks Troy.

"You're going to plead guilty."

"Like hell I am. I didn't do it."

Mathias laughs. "Another innocent man. Well, join the club. Every prison I've ever been in is full of innocent men."

"Well I'm another one," says Troy.

"I'm glad to hear it but the judge is going to find that a bit hard to believe with that cop's blood all over you and the murder weapon in your hand."

"That cop knocked me out before I could tell him what happened."

"I suppose you're going to tell me that you were out taking a run when you heard a shot. Then some punk kid came running around the corner and wiped blood all over you and shoved the gun in your hand."

Troy is surprised. "Actually I was walking my dog but that's basically what happened."

"Do you have any idea how that's going to sound in court? Why don't you save us all a lot of trouble and plead guilty."

"Plead guilty to killing a cop?"

"The blood on your clothes and the gun in your hand and the witness who saw you is a long time cop. Do I have to paint you any more of a picture? What do you want me to do? Put your dog on the witness stand?"

"Tiger got spooked with the gunshot. He ran off down the street. If I was going to shoot someone would I take my dog with me?"

Mathias looks at his watch. "I gotta go. I'll be back when you've thought about what I said."

"Don't come back until you're prepared to listen to what I say."

"I heard. Your argument is that you wouldn't take your dog if you were going to kill someone. Won't wash! Looks like premeditation."

"I won't plead guilty to something I didn't do. Anyway who's paying you?"

"I told you. I'm doing this out of the goodness of my heart. This is the United States of Assholes. Didn't you know? All cop killers get a free lawyer. Look I'm doing you a favor. Now do me one and plead guilty and I'm out of here."

"Don't you even want to know what happened?"

"I'm your lawyer. I don't need to know what happened. I'm sure you had a good reason. I've come close to killing cops myself."

"I didn't do it, you got that."

On his way out of the prison Black Jack catches up to Mathias. "He won't cop a guilty plea. Says he didn't do it."

"Then you just better lose, Matthew. You just better lose."

"It's Mathias, asshole."

"Yeah, you told me already."

"Why didn't you just blow him away on the street? Isn't that what you usually do?"

"Don't you fuck with me, asshole! You could have a nasty accident."

SABIA - AUSTRALIA

Sabia has been fighting with herself about allowing Rose to be tested as a possible donor. Half of her is relieved that she found Rose – or that Rose found her. The other half of her feels guilty about

Rose undergoing the tests that could save her life especially as Rose is not well herself. Regardless of her inner battle, Sabia is grateful that Rose has agreed to help. And it has also given the doctors an opportunity to examine Rose and take some action to treat her breathing problems.

Sitting on Rose's hospital bed Sabia waits for the results of the tests which will tell her whether she has found her answer. She looks at her watch. How much longer will she have to wait to find out if she is to be reprieved? Just as she looks up she sees Dr Kelligan who is accompanied by the specialist Dr Ambrose. She notes the wrinkle moving across Dr Kelligan's brow and her heart sinks but she is determined to keep her spirits up especially in the presence of Rose. She forces a smile and says brightly: "So what's the good news, Doctors?"

Dr Ambrose takes the lead. "I wish it were good news, Sabia."

Rose is as anxious as Sabia to hear the results of her tests. "My daughter, my Sabia, she'll be alright now - with my blood?"

Dr Ambrose doesn't answer immediately and Dr Kelligan leans across and picks up Rose's chart.

"What is it? " asks Sabia. "Aren't we a match?"

"I wish I had better news for you both but I'm afraid not. Rose is not a match, Sabia. I'm sorry," says Dr Ambrose.

Rose sits up quickly. "But my Sabia is my daughter, you know that she is. My blood can't cure her?"

"I'm sorry Rose," says Dr Kelligan. "Sabia may be your daughter but we need a different kind of match for a donor. But we have worked out a regimen to manage your emphysema and the pharmacy will shortly be sending up your prescriptions. We'd like to keep you here in hospital for a few more days for observation." Sabia smiles at Rose. "Well that's good news at least."

But Rose is anxious to get home – back to the quiet of the bush. After they pick up Rose's prescriptions, the two women leave the hospital. Sabia is overcome by a strong feeling of depression. Though she had not wanted to put Rose through any more trauma, she had to admit to herself that she was hoping that Rose would be a match and that her search for a donor would have been over. She knows that the future is no longer assured for her and she pushes those thoughts to the back of her mind as she tries to concentrate on "one step at a time".

Sabia knows she can never make up for what Rose has been through but she would like to mark the occasion of their re-connection in some way. She feels that a significant present for Rose would have to be something practical and useful and then she remembers the chain of outback outfitters that has been a legend in Australia for more than 50 years. A trip to the store Sabia decides is what they both need. It will cheer them up and it will provide a fitting present for Rose, who is quiet and introspective as they drive to the store. Once inside, Sabia tries on a pair of hand-made leather boots while the shop assistant gives her a strong sales pitch. "These boots are hand-made. It takes one man four weeks to make one pair. They are the only boots in the world that are made from one piece of leather. They were originally made for stockmen who ride and work in the outback. Now even models and movie stars wear them. These are made from kangaroo skin. It's the strongest leather for its weight in the world."

Sabia is determined to buy her newly found Aboriginal mother a pair of the special boots. She hasn't broached the subject with Rose but she wants to convince her to stay in the city.

For her part, Rose is always overwhelmed by the city. The noise, the people, the movement and the traffic always remind her of a cattle stampede and she feels an underlying danger whenever she is in the city.

Sabia picks out a pair of black kangaroo skin boots and encourages Rose to try them on.

"These are two good for me, Sabia. Save your money."

"Please," says Sabia. "I want you to have them." Rose relents and tries on the boots. They are a perfect fit.

As they leave the shop – both wearing their new boots - they pass by an electrical appliance store. Its whole window is taken up by TVs that are all turned to the news. The news item running is about Troy's trial. The report catches Rose's attention. She stops. And then she sees Troy. Tears start to roll down her face.

Sabia is shocked to see Rose crying. "What is it? Are you alright, Rose?"

"That's your brother - that's Troy."

The newsreader says that Troy's trial will begin in three weeks. As Sabia and Rose start to walk away from the store window the news continues with an item about the impending transport strike. "The Transport Workers Union's federal executive today rejected the latest offer by employers in their wage dispute and called a strike from midnight tonight."

SUZY - USA

On the other side of the world Suzy is out of bed dancing with her bunny. The overhead TV is on and she sees the same news report about Troy that Sabia has just seen in Australia. Suzy is horrified when she hears the news. "That's Troy! It's not true. Troy wouldn't do bad things." Mrs Lopez had told her that Troy wouldn't be able to come and see her at the hospital for the time being but she had not told Suzy the details of the trouble Troy is in.

MATHIAS - USA

Mathias walks through the door of a bar as the band is playing a deep blues number. He nods to the singer/guitarist Fox, then sits down and orders. "Whisky. Double."

The bartender has come to expect trouble when Mathias is in the bar. He warns him. "No trouble tonight, or you'll be out on your ass."

Mathias holds up his hands as if to show that he will comply. "Just a quiet drink, that's all I'm after." The bartender slides the glass down the bar and Mathias almost misses catching it.

The band finishes the song and stops for a break. Fox comes over to Mathias. They are pleased to see each other. Fox slaps Mathias on the back. "What's shakin' Bro."

"Lookin' good," says Mathias.

Some people don't need to do any explaining to each other. From the first minute they meet there is an instant connection that goes deep and is everlasting. That depth of feeling is like a concrete foundation between Mathias and Fox. Neither of them can remember where or how they met. Their friendship goes back to their teenage years and the understated animosity between them when Fox was called up for duty in Vietnam but Mathias missed out. Mathias later admits and Fox agrees wholeheartedly that the army actually got it right. Fox was the better choice for a fighting man. Mathias would have been at a loss in uniform. Fox shone during his service, outshining his peers. Though he was awarded several medals during the war, he never bothered to collect them. At army headquarters Fox's file is still marked M.I.A. – missing in action. Fox has never bothered to try to find out why his file is marked thus and has certainly never bothered to correct it. He lives outside society with no known address and no way for any authority to track him. He likes it like that. His link to the world of normality is through Mathias who provides a barrier between Fox and authority. It has been an admirable arrangement that has suited them both. In his legal career Mathias has found his friendship with Fox invaluable using him like his own personal ninja for information gathering and other somewhat nefarious activities the details of which shall remain cloaked in secrecy known only to the two of them. A love of blues is another trait they share and Mathias is often in the audience when Fox comes out of his forest lair to light up the night sky with his aggressive and colorful guitar riffs.

TROY – US PRISON

Father O'Brien was shocked and disbelieving when he learnt that Troy had been charged with murder. He was sure that Troy was innocent and he felt strongly that the situation had come about in some way as a result of Troy training young boxers. 'I wish he had listened to me,' he thinks but realizes that thinking thus will not help Troy so he immediately organizes a prayer vigil for Troy and, as soon as he can get away from his priestly duties he visits Troy in his cell. "What do you need me to do, Troy?"

"Nothing, Father. There is nothing you or anyone can do."

"There must be something I can do for you besides prayer."

"No-one will ever believe I didn't do it."

"You know who did though, don't you?"

"I can't tell anyone," says Troy.

The priest shakes his head. "Not even to save yourself?"

"No, Father." Troy stands up and stretches, walks to the slit in the door and looks through as if he is checking to see that no-one is there. "Do you believe in payback, Father?"

"What do you mean, Troy?"

"You know - like the bible says: "What you sow, so shall ye reap."

Father O'Brien is puzzled by Troy's remark. "I wouldn't call that payback. That's just the golden rule. Treat everyone as you want to be treated yourself. You know, do the right thing."

Troy sits down again. "I can't sleep for the nightmares."

The priest is anxious to provide some consolation and support to Troy. "Nightmares? I would think that is perfectly normal after all you've been through. Often dreams help you make sense of traumatic events."

"These are about when I was in 'nam."

"You've never told me you were in the service." Now the priest's puzzlement is heightened.

"I've tried hard to forget it," says Troy, rubbing his face as if to wipe out the memories.

"What are your dreams about?"

"What happened - over there."

"War truly is hell, hell on earth."

"Father, I'm wondering if I'm being paid back for what I did."

"You fought for your country like every other soldier."

Troy is quiet. Father O'Brien is ready to hear a confession. "Tell me about Vietnam, Troy."

Troy suddenly begins to get agitated. He paces around the cell. "I didn't mean to do it. I just didn't see them." Father O'Brien waits quietly. "We were caught in an ambush. Someone threw a grenade at us. I took some shrapnel in the leg. I fired - blindly in the direction that the grenade had come from. When the shooting stopped I went to see who had thrown it." He hesitates as if he is reliving the scene. "They were kids, Father. No more than 4 or 5 years old. Kids! And I killed them - both. They were lying there together - a brother and sister."

Father O'Brien searches for the right words. He doesn't want to come out with some meaningless platitude so he stays quiet listening to Troy.

"Kids, Father. Little kids. I'll never forget their faces. I dream about them every night."

The priest replies in a measured tone. "I don't have any glib answers for you, Troy. We are simply human beings, not gods. We're not perfect. All we can do is the best with what we're given. No-one can expect more."

Troy sits down on the bed once more.

"Maybe that lawyer is right."

"What do you mean?" Father O'Brien is puzzled.

"I should plead guilty."

"But you didn't do it?"

"No, but I can't give him up, Father. He's just a kid."

SABIA - AUSTRALIA

Sabia is very anxious to get to America. Although she is not licensed to practise law there she hopes that she will be able to be of some assistance to the lawyer representing Troy. She needs to bring him back to Australia in the hope that he will be a donor match. It's a long shot she realizes. She has to convince the US authorities that she is related to Troy. That will be hard. She knows that is just the first hurdle. Then she will have to convince Troy to help her. She doesn't remember anything about their long ago relationship and Troy might not remember her or even want to remember her. Even if he agrees to be tested as a donor, how will she accomplish that when he is locked up in prison but she quickly puts that out of her mind. She knows she has an enormous task and going over it in her mind is not going to make it any easier. "Take it one step at a time," she tells herself. First she must try to contact the prison authorities. Sabia dials the prison number. She doesn't think that they will allow her to speak to Troy immediately but she is hoping to at least get a message to him.

The phone rings in the prison and is answered by a guard. Sabia is nervous and her throat constricts making her voice faint. "I'd like to speak to the warden please. I'm calling from Australia."

"Australia?" The guard is surprised.

"Please tell him I'm a lawyer. I'm calling about Troy Washington."

"The warden's busy."

"It's urgent. Please put me through. I'm his sister."

"Sister! Listen sister, that asshole doesn't have any sisters or brothers or any known relatives." He slams down the phone.

Sabia hears the line go dead. "You bastard!" She knows it is useless to call the prison again at least until the next change of guards. Try another tack. She starts dialing again.

In Mathias' office he has passed out on his desk with an almost empty bottle of whisky at his elbow. The ringing of the phone disturbs him. He stirs - slightly. Seeming to have a mind of its own his hand moves toward the phone knocking the whisky bottle to the floor. The crash half wakes him. He opens one eye, sees rather than hears the phone ringing, puts his head back down on the desk and pushes the phone over the edge into the wastepaper bin.

At her end Sabia hears the phone answered then hears a crash and the phone cuts out. She shouts into the receiver. "Answer the phone damn you!"

TROY – US PRISON

Meanwhile Troy is alone in his cell unaware of Sabia's efforts to reach him. But he is never really alone. A guard leans into the slot of the door of his cell. "Hey! Cocksucker! You can't hide. I'll be back. You won't know when."

SABIA – AUSTRALIA

Having given up on trying to reach anyone by phone, Sabia is at Perth Airport trying to get a flight to the US. As she walks into the airport building she is confronted with pandemonium. The airport is jampacked with travellers. She joins a line which seems endless and stationary. After several minutes she decides to confront one of the airport people in uniform. "What's going on? I need to get to the US. It's urgent."

The airport staff member is sympathetic as he explains to Sabia that there are no flights leaving because of the transport strike. "No fuel, no flights," he says.

"But this is an emergency," says Sabia desperately.

He smiles at her and gestures at all the people waiting. "I'm sure it is but so are these – they all have emergencies too. I'm sorry but you'll just have to wait your turn. We'll get you on a flight as soon as we can."

"When can I expect that to be?"

"Whenever this strike is over."

"You don't understand my brother's in trouble in America. I've got to get there."

"I'm very sorry, Miss, but my hands are tied. We're trying to make the best of it. Everyone just has to take their turn. Be thankful that you have a home to go to while you wait. These people have been sleeping here in the airport."

"But this is a matter of life and death."

"There really isn't anything I can do. You'll just have to wait like everybody else."

Sabia finally gives up and walks away from the desk. She spots an international phone booth. This time she is successful at getting through to Mathias.

He wonders why he always seems to attract the nuts. "You're his sister? But you're Australian and he's American." Sabia tries to explain about Troy and her background but she feels strongly that Mathias is not interested.

"You were taken away as children?" queries Mathias, disbelieving.

Sabia goes into the background of the stolen generation children trying to get Mathias to understand what happened to her and Troy.

"You haven't seen him since you were three. Exactly how many years ago was that?"

"Thirty."

When Sabia hears Mathias repeat "thirty" back to her she finally realizes that he is not going to take her seriously. There is a pause in the conversation and then Mathias says: "Why don't you call me again when you're feeling better" and he hangs up.

Sabia has to admit to herself that it does sound like a wild tale and she is not really surprised that he hung up even though she is desperate to work out some way of helping Troy so she can bring him home to Australia.

TROY – US PRISON

While Troy is lying awake on the hard prison mattress, a prison guard takes a stiff piece of rubber hose out of his locker. Rubber hose leaves no bruises. Troy sits up on alert as he hears the guard's boots echoing down the corridor.

He can tell they are getting closer as he picks them out amongst the rapping on the metal doors by other prisoners who know what the guard is about to do. They beat a rhythmic warning to Troy as the boots echo down the corridor in a harsh and strident tone. Troy doesn't need the message. He knows the guard is on the way to him. He's not going to the local dance, that's for sure. All along the corridor through their cell doors the adjacent prisoners can hear the muffled thuds as the guard administers a beating to Troy.

SUZY - USA

At 9 years old Suzy also knows about beatings. In her young life she has seen much of the harsh side of life, the side of life that no 9-year old should ever see. Life has not been kind to her so the day that Troy walked into her hospital room was a day of joy for Suzy. She considers Troy her one true friend, the kind of friend that she can count on. She feels that she knows what Troy is capable of and Suzy knows that Troy is not a killer. She wants her friend Troy to know that he can count on her at this dark time, so she is sitting on her bed writing a letter. A nurse comes in to check on her and asks Suzy if she is writing to her parents.

"I don't have any parents," says Suzy.

"So the letter's to one of your friends?"

"Troy's my only friend," says Suzy. "He's in trouble. I'm writing to the judge. What should I put? Dear Judge?"

"I think you should say: Your Honor".

Suzy continues with her letter.

The nurse reads over her shoulder. "Dear Your

Honor. Troy is a good man. He wouldn't kill anybody. Please let him go. I miss him very much." Then Suzy looks up at the nurse again. "Should I say: Love, Suzy?"

"Maybe: Sincerely, Suzy," says the nurse.

Suzy writes carefully. "Sincerely Suzy." She folds the letter and puts it in an envelope. "Now," says Suzy. "A letter for Troy."

The nurse asks her if she wants her to mail the letters for her but Suzy has plans of her own. "No thanks."

TROY – US PRISON

The next morning Troy is alone in one corner of the prison exercise yard. As he walks, it is obvious he's in pain but he has no visible bruises. He leans against the yard wall when other prisoners, in ones and twos, come over to him. One offers him a cigarette. Troy has never been a smoker so he refuses the offer. Joey is the prison wiseguy. He knows how everything works and who to keep in with and who to avoid. He has decided to take Troy under his wing. "You don't smoke 'em, they're good as gold in here. They're money. Buy what you want."

Troy is guarded. "Don't have use for much."

Joey is not to be denied. "Little something to get you up. Little something to get you down."

"Don't need it," says Troy.

"Hey, one less cop benefits us all."

Troy is determined that Joey should know he is innocent. "I didn't do it."

Joey smirks. "Welcome to the 21st Chapter of the Prison Academy of Choir Boys. We're all innocent."

Troy tries to smile at the joke but it's too painful. He grimaces.

Joey understands. He heard the noises in the night. "You had a visitor last night."

Troy nods.

"Bastard had his friend with him - the one that doesn't leave any marks."

Troy does not want to be drawn into any discussion of the prison guards.

"He's a sadistic bastard but I've got a little surprise for him," says Joey.

Troy is anxious not to discuss it. He has noticed Joey's teardrop tattoos under his eye. "Interesting tattoos. Do they mean anything?" Joey points to the first one which is an open tattoo. "This one's for Tashawn. Like a bro he was. Growing up I was round his Ma's more than mine."

"So it's so that you remember him?" asks Troy.

"So people know we was like bros, feel me."

The next one is filled in – a dark spot in the middle of the two open tattoos. Joey points to it. "This one, this black one, that's for the asshole who murdered Tashawn."

"What happened to Tashawn?"

"Shot by a cop resisting arrest, 'cept he wasn't resisting anything."

"Sorry to hear that," says Troy.

Joey grins. "But I got the bastard. That's why I'm here."

"You killed a cop?"

Joey grins. "Just like you."

"But I ….." Troy decides not to protest his innocence again.

"Bastard wasted Tashawn so I wasted him. Had to. Made his Ma a promise. Had to keep it."

Troy does not want to ask about the third teardrop but Joey's in the mood to talk. "This one's a promise for that bastard screw that bashed you."

"Why?"

"I owe him."

"Don't do anything for me."

"It's not for you – he's had it coming from all of us for a long time. He's a snitch. Turned me in to the warden."

Troy walks away. He realizes that being seen in Joey's company can only do him harm.

SUZY – USA

Looking over her shoulder Suzy inches down the corridor into the elevator. Whenever she sees someone coming, she ducks into a vacant toilet.

Coming out of the elevator she bends down to creep past the counter where the guard is so that she can slip out the front door without being seen. She makes it successfully to the bus stop near the hospital. A bus pulls up and she gets in. She shows a piece of paper to the bus driver who nods and drives off.

MATHIAS – USA

Meanwhile, Mathias has his feet up on his desk. He is reading the sports pages - racing guide - of the daily newspaper. He looks around puzzled as there is a soft tapping at his door. Without bothering to look up he calls out: "Yeah." There is no answer. Still he doesn't look up. "It's open." Slowly the door opens a crack, then it slowly opens fully. A nose comes round the door and it is followed by the rest of Suzy's face. "Scuse me, Mister," says Suzy.

Mathias is surprised at the young voice. He finally looks up from his paper, sliding his feet off the table when he sees his young visitor. "You lost?"

"Are you Mr Swinburn?" asks Suzy.

"Swinebourne. Who wants to know?" says Mathias puzzled. For a brief moment he wonders whether this girl may be one of his children come to find their father. He does a quick inventory of any girlfriends he had years ago who may have had children with him that he doesn't know about.

Suzy is not put off by his manner. "I do. I'm looking for you."

"What did I do? Run over your cat?" He points to the sofa. "Sit down -- err?"

"Suzy."

"Well Suzy. Does your mother know where you are?"

"I don't have one."

"Your father?"

"They took me away from him. He hurt me. I only have Troy."

"Ahah," says Mathias. "So you know Troy."

Suzy is getting upset at the thought of Troy being locked up. "Yes, and I know he didn't do what they said on the news. You've got to save him. Troy's a good man."

Mathias is starting to soften a bit in spite of himself. "Well Suzy, that's what I'm trying to do. How do you know Troy?"

"He comes and reads to me in hospital."

"How long have you been in hospital?"

"This is my fourth time."

Mathias is shocked. "Four times?"

"Every time my daddy hurts me. This time I don't have to go back home.

"Troy says they are going to find me a new family - with a mother, but I really want to have Troy for a father."

Mathias gets up from his office chair and goes over to sit next to Suzy on the sofa. She digs into her pocket bringing out the two letters. "I wrote to the judge. Will you give it to him?"

"You wrote to the judge?" Matthias is intrigued at someone so young being so mature. "I'll see that he gets it," he says taking the letter.

Suzy hands him the second letter. "And this one's for Troy. I miss him." And then Suzy does something that really floors Mathias. She leans across and kisses him on the cheek. Mathias tries to regain his composure. "Who brought you here today?"

"I brought myself."

"You came all this way by yourself?"

"Well, the lady driving the bus really brought me here from the hospital. And I should go back now, so they won't know I'm not there."

"Come on, Miss Suzy. I'll drive you back." Suzy takes hold of Mathias' hand as they walk through the carpark to his car.

TROY – US PRISON

The next day Mathias visits Troy. He hands Troy Suzy's letter. "Had a visit from one of your friends."

"Oh," says Troy.

"Young Suzy."

"Is she all right? There's nothing wrong is there?" Troy is worried about her.

"No," says Mathias. "She's worried about you. She's really something for someone so young. Have you thought any more about your plea?"

"I told you before. I didn't do it."

"That's not going to do you any good unless you can finger who did."

"You should ask that crooked cop, Black Jack."

"He's the main witness against you. A veteran cop. His testimony will be hard to refute. The jury has a predilection for believing cops. They don't want to think that the force is corrupt."

After Mathias has left, Troy reads Suzy's letter. "Remember the rainbow, Troy. Remember the rainbow." Troy drops the letter and smacks the wall with his fist. He knows there will be no more rainbows for him and none for Jason.

Should he plead guilty and get it over with? He's had a fair run. He's 35 years old. That's longer than some people have.

One thing Troy is sure of, he can't give up Jason. Troy knows that the police chief is pushing to have his case jump the ticket and be in court in the next two weeks. The mayor has been bringing pressure to bear as well. He's up for re-election.

Mathias is another source of pressure. "It's an open and shut case. It will look better if you plead guilty. They might consider life rather than the death penalty."

Troy knows that is a lie. As a 'cop killer' he knows he's facing the death penalty. He's also very worried about Jason and has tried to reach him. He has been using his precious prison phone calls to call Jimmy's Gym. "Nobody's seen him since you got arrested," says Jimmy.

"When you see him, tell him I want to talk to him."

FOX – USA

After his visit to the prison, Mathias drives out to see Fox. He gets out of his car and walks through the forest until he is sweating. He stops for a breather and leans against a tree. Suddenly, WHOOSH! Fox drops down out of the tree almost on top of Mathias. "Shit! Give me a fuckin' heart attack!"

Fox laughs. "Just wanted to see if you have one."

Mathias grumbles. "Don't know why you wanted me to come all the way out here."

"To get some of that city pollution out of your head." Fox steers Mathias further through the forest until they break through the trees to a clearing where there is a small lake. They start to walk along the lakeside but Mathias is not even looking at it. He is studying his shoes as if he is ashamed to look Fox in the face. "Ever have any doubts about things you do?" he asks Fox.

"Plenty, Bro. Wouldn't be human if you didn't. What particular doubts are you having?"

Mathias pauses. "Maybe I misjudged him. Maybe he didn't kill that cop."

"Does it matter? Don't you always throw your guts into it whether they're guilty or not?"

Mathias is quiet. "He's going to plead guilty."

Fox is surprised. "When did he decide that?"

"He hasn't yet but he will."

"You happy about that?"

"It's a case of I have to be."

"That doesn't sound like you. You usually do just what you want."

"Backed into a corner this time."

"Anything you need me to do to get you out of that corner?" asks Fox.

"Thanks, but no thanks. I need to sort this out myself."

JASON – USA

Keesha has brought some food to Jason who has been hiding in a derelict building. She climbs up onto the roof where Jason is sitting on some cardboard boxes. While Jason eats hungrily Keesha is standing up looking at the view. Suddenly her attention is caught by something. She ducks down. "Sssshhhh! A car!" Through a hole in the wall they can see a car creeping slowly onto the property down an overgrown lane at the back. Jason recognizes the car. "That's Black Jack's car! We've got to get out of here."

Keesha takes command. "He'll see us. Stay down. I know what to do." There are some loose bricks near them. Keesha picks up one.

Down in the laneway Black Jack gets out of the car just as Keesha takes careful aim. She throws the brick which hits Black Jack on the side of his head. He is knocked off his feet and he falls back against his car, one arm at a crazy angle near the door handle. His body slides to the ground but his arm is still bent up near the handle. Jason is amazed at Keesha who looks completely calm as if she had done nothing. She grabs Jason's elbow. "Now we can leave." They have to squeeze past Black Jack's car to escape. Jason tries to shepherd Keesha past Black Jack but Keesha stops to look. "He's still breathing." Jason is anxious to get Keesha away from there. "Keesha, come on!"

"Wait a minute Jason."

"He'll wake up and kill us," says Jason.

Keesha pulls Black Jack's handcuffs off his belt and expertly cuffs his arm to the doorhandle. "Let's see him explain this," she says grinning at Jason.

TROY – US PRISON

While Sabia is prevented from flying to New York to help Troy because of the transport strike which has grounded all aircraft, she has been on the phone to anyone and everyone she can think of to get help for Troy. Her constant badgering of the Australian Consul General's office in New York has not gone unnoticed. Finally it is agreed to send someone from the office to visit Troy in an effort to stop Sabia's phone calls.

The Consul General has requested information from Australia about Troy's background as Sabia has insisted that he is her long-lost brother and, as an Australian, he should be getting support from the consular officials in New York.

Though there has been no confirmation from Australia that Troy was, in fact, born there, the Consul General sends one of his officers to visit Troy. Sitting opposite the official in the jail's visiting room, Troy is surprised when he learns that the official is from the Australian consulate.

"How did you know I was here?" he asks.

"There's some crazy lady lawyer from Perth ringing us every few hours to do something for you."

"What's her name?" asks Troy.

"Are you saying that you were actually born in Australia?" asks the official. He begins to take an interest. Up till now he thought he was just on a futile errand. "Her name's Sabia Malone. She says she's your sister."

"Sabia," Troy says to himself. "I don't recognize the 'Malone' but my little sister's name was Sabia. They took us away when we were very young."

"But you've lived here all your life? Are you a citizen? How did you get here?" Suddenly the official is interested. He takes out a pen and legal pad from his briefcase.

"So your name is Troy Washington? Was Washington the name of your Australian parents?"

"No, Myrtle and Eric Washington were the parents I grew up with."

"How did you end up with them if they were Americans?"

"They were missionaries in Australia back then." Troy explains to the official that he and Sabia were split up when they were taken from their mother, Rose. The children were placed in separate church missions. The Washingtons were visiting one of the missions on their way back to their home in New York. They took a shine to Troy and just before they left the mission they asked him if he wanted to have a ride in their car. Of course Troy agreed, he loved anything mechanical especially cars. Once he was inside the car Mr Washington just kept driving. They never took him back to the mission. Next thing Troy remembered was being on a plane and then all his memories were of his childhood in New York.

"So, in fact you were stolen twice," says the official. "Once from your mother and then from the mission."

Troy had never thought about it like that. "I guess so," he says.

"What about documents?"

"Well the army took care of that when they sent me to 'nam."

"Do you have a copy of your birth certificate?"

"No, I've never had one."

"You have legal representation for your court case?"

"I guess he's a court appointed lawyer. He doesn't seem too interested in my case though. Wants me to plead guilty."

"Do you want another lawyer?"

"That won't make any difference to the outcome."

"So you're saying you did it. You shot that cop."

"No, that's not what I'm saying. I didn't but it won't make any difference."

"Do you know who did it?"

Troy turns away. "Let's just leave things as they are."

After the consular official's visit to Troy, he is sitting at his desk going over the notes he made about Troy's case when the Consul General walks in.

"What did you think? Is he credible?" They both discuss Troy and his situation. There has been no confirmation from Australia as to Troy's nationality because there is no trace of Troy and he wasn't able to furnish them with his original surname. Though the consular official feels that Troy's story is credible, the Consul-General decides that there is nothing further they can do to help him.

BLACK JACK – USA

After the humiliation of Black Jack being found passed out and handcuffed to his car he is placed on leave pending an inquiry. He decides to put more pressure on Mathias. They meet in the same underground bar as before.

The meeting is tense and the other bar patrons feel the negative vibes and leave. The bartender also makes himself scarce. He has had previous experience with Black Jack and he does not want to be in the firing line if he loses his temper.

Mathias is especially edgy because he can see Black Jack's house of cards about to fall and he knows it will take him with it, ending Mathias' legal career.

Black Jack stands over Mathias who is sitting on a bar stool nursing a whisky. "That asshole's going to plead guilty. Right."

Mathias takes his time replying. "Nothing right about it."

"Then you better make sure you lose, asshole."

"You already told me."

Black Jack grabs Mathias and lifts him up off the barstool. "You win and you're a dead man." He drops Mathias back onto the stool and storms out.

Mathias is shaken even though he tries not to show it to the barman who has returned.

JASON – USA

Jason knows he is taking a huge risk to appear on the streets where he knows Black Jack will be looking for him – no doubt even more enraged than normal after his encounter with the brick Keesha threw even though Black Jack doesn't know that Jason and Keesha were involved in his humiliating handcuffing. But Jason is determined to speak to Troy and try to explain what happened. He feels he owes him that much at least. He walks down a dark back street all hunched up with a hat pulled down almost to his chin.

He sticks to the shadows hoping to be as inconspicuous as possible. Turning a corner he sees what he has been looking for - a deserted phone booth. Jason picks up the phone, all the time looking back over his shoulder. He is very nervous. He doesn't know it but Keesha has followed him. She hides in a nearby building as he enters the phone booth.

From the tiny window of his cell Troy is trying to see any stars that might be in the sky. His reverie is interrupted by a guard banging on his cell door.

"Get your sorry ass out here. There's a phone call for you." As Troy answers the phone the guard stands almost on top of him. He hisses: "Two minutes asshole so talk quick."

Troy immediately recognizes Jason's voice. "Why didn't you turn me in, Mr Troy? They're going to kill you, Mr Troy."

"Looks that way."

"They gonna electrocute you, Mr Troy. You gonna let them do that? For me? And Black Jack - he's gonna kill me. Maybe it's better I tell them. I'm the only one knows what happened."

"So what happened, Jason?"

"He said he'd rape my mother if I didn't do it, Mr Troy. I'm sorry. Your lawyer's his man, Mr Troy. Just ask him."

A dark-clothed arm holding a pistol appears in the phone booth. Jason sees the gun out of the corner of his eye. Bang! Jason falls to the floor of the phone booth. The gun and the hand disappear. The phone is dangling, swinging over Jason's crumpled body. The sound of the gun going off travels down the phone line. Troy is alarmed for Jason. He shouts into the phone. "Jason! Jason! Are you there!" The prison guard reaches across and hangs up the phone. "He might be there asshole but you're not. I said two minutes. Well your two minutes are up!"

KEESHA – USA

The yellow glow from a street light shows the face of Jason's killer for a split second as Keesha watches from the adjacent building. She recognizes that face. Though she is desperate to get to Jason she knows she must wait until the shooter has climbed into his car and driven away or she will be in danger too. Just as she is about to run to Jason, an ambulance arrives. The paramedics load Jason into the ambulance and rush him away. She knows they will take Jason to Harlem Hospital and she runs down the street to Cheyenne's apartment. She quietly opens the door. "It's me, Cheyenne."

"Keesha, I've been so worried. Where's Jason?"

Keesha breaks down as she tells Cheyenne about Jason's shooting. She helps Cheyenne get dressed so they can go to the hospital and see him. She tells Cheyenne that she saw who shot Jason as she was hiding in a building just near the telephone booth. Cheyenne is angry and upset at the same time. "You must go to the police and tell them what you know."

"You don't understand. It's the police who shot Jason."

With Keesha leading the way the two women arrive at the hospital. The receptionist will only tell them that Jason is in surgery. She points to the waiting room and tells them to wait but Keesha has never been one to do as she's told.

She helps Cheyenne walk down the corridor telling the protesting receptionist that they need to find the bathroom.

Following the signs Keesha finds the surgery wing. A surgeon comes out of one of the rooms and Keesha takes the opportunity to ask about Jason.

"The young man who was shot?"

"Yes," says Keesha. "This is his mother and we're trying to find out how he is."

The surgeon can see that Cheyenne is not well so she leads them both to chairs nearby. "I'll see what I can find out."

After an achingly long five minutes the surgeon comes out to tell them that Jason is still in surgery. It could be a long wait and she advises them to go home but the two women are determined not to leave. Several hours later they are both asleep leaning against each other as another doctor comes to tell them that they can now go in and see Jason but just for a minute or two.

"Will he be all right, doctor? Will he live?" Cheyenne begs for an answer.

"I won't lie to you. It's touch and go. The gunshot did a lot of damage. We've only been able to repair some of it. It's too soon to tell."

Keesha helps Cheyenne as they enter Jason's darkened room. They lean close in to him listening to his breathing. Cheyenne is relieved to hear that he is still breathing so there is some hope. Keesha pulls a chair over close to the bed so Cheyenne can sit down. She is shocked by all the equipment that surrounds Jason and watching the dials and switches wonders which one is attached to his heart. As the dawn light starts to inch through the window Cheyenne notices Jason start to move his head a little.

"Jason, I'm here." He opens one eye slightly. Speaking almost inaudibly he says: "I'm sorry Mom."

"Shhh, don't talk, save your strength," says Cheyenne. Keesha leans a little closer to the bed. She wants Jason to see that she is there but he closes his eyes again.

As Cheyenne rubs Jason's hand he opens his eyes again. "Black Jack made me do it, Mom. He said he would rape you if I didn't." Then he lapses into sleep again.

Cheyenne is puzzled. "Who's Black Jack and what did he make Jason do?"

The nurse returns and ushers them out. "I'm sorry but you'll have to leave."

Just as they reach the door, Jason opens his eyes and says: "I love you Mom." Then his eyes close and the heart monitor alarm goes off. Cheyenne sees the flat line that tells her that her son has gone.

TROY – US PRISON

The next day Troy is working in the laundry room of the prison. He's not certain that Jason is dead but feels that after the gunshot he heard through the phone that there is every likelihood that he is. He realizes that there is no hope that he will not be held to account for the death of Sargeant Strong so, making sure that the guard does not see him, he slips a pillowcase up his sleeve. Troy has decided to make a rope.

That evening Mathias tries again to convince Troy to plead guilty. Troy is furious to think that he is being railroaded, that people over whom he has no control are hell-bent on taking his life from him.

"I know you're working for Black Jack. That's who is pressuring you to get me to plead guilty isn't it?"

"Who told you that?"

"A little bird."

"Well they're wrong. The court appointed me your lawyer," says Mathias, his face reddening.

"Yeah and Black Jack convinced the court that you would be a good choice. What's he got over you? What do you owe him? Did he take care of some rival in the past and now he's leant on you to get me convicted. Case closed. Door shut on Troy Washington. And Black Jack is free to keep running his rackets and killing his rivals."

"Yeah he's no Santa Claus. But no-one tells me what to do."

"Who do you think you're kidding, Mathias? Not me. That's for sure. My goose is cooked and you're turning up the hot knob on Black Jack's stove."

SABIA - USA

The strike is finally over in Australia and Sabia is at last able to fly to America - and Troy. She is not a person to waste time so she goes direct from the airport to Mathias' office. Sabia paces around Mathias' office while he watches her.

He leans back in his chair with a look of disdain on his face. 'Who is this crazy woman?' he thinks. 'She's good looking - yes. Sexy - yes. But who is she and what does she want?' He doesn't want to know, doesn't want to be pulled into her mad scheme whatever it is.

"I know it sounds like an unlikely story but it's true," says Sabia realizing that Mathias is not really listening to her.

"But how do you know he's your brother?"

"I just know. That's all."

"It's very sweet of you to fall in love with a condemned man. Happens all the time. Women even marry men on death row. Different strokes, I guess. And it's very heroic of you to fly over here to rescue him - just like some knight on a white donkey - but this is real life, Girly."

Sabia flies at him grabbing him by the shirtfront, almost knocking him off his chair. "Listen Mate! If you ever patronize me again I'll knock your front teeth so far down your throat that you'll be cleaning your teeth with your toothbrush stuck up your arse! I don't care whether you believe I'm his sister or not. You're not important to me, Troy is. And I don't believe that any brother of mine - regardless of the fact that we've been apart for thirty years - would commit murder. That's just not in our blood." Sabia suddenly realizes what she is doing. She stops, steps back. "I'm sorry.......it was a long flight."

"I thought you would kill me for a minute."

Sabia regains her composure. "What kind of defence are you going to present?"

"The dead cop's blood on his clothing and the gun in his hand will be hard to dispute. The only witness was Black Jack – a cop. Who do you think the jury will believe? The victim's blood and the gun that killed him. And his cop partner who was an eyewitness. That's pretty persuasive."

"What about this other person? The bloke at the consulate seems to think he's covering up for someone."

"If there was someone else, why would he protect them? We're talking about his life. I don't buy it. Nor would any jury. Understandable. If there was someone else he would have named them."

"Well I need Troy. If he's a match to me, he's my only hope."

"Hope for what?"

"I need a bone marrow transfusion from a relative. I have leukaemia. And Troy is my last shot."

"I don't think that's gonna spring him."

"We'll appeal."

"On what grounds?"

"We've got to find whoever he's protecting. What have you done about that?"

"So this is about you, not about Troy."

Sabia starts to get angry again. "Of course it's about Troy and me and our mother who is about to die in Australia. You need to get your arse moving and find whoever it is that Troy is protecting. There's only a week until his trial." She bangs her fist on Mathias' desk. "What are you doing to find him?"

"As a matter of fact I've got someone out looking for him right now."

Mathias is still very dubious about Sabia but he agrees to drive her to the prison and see if the warden will agree to her seeing Troy. If the warden thinks she is credible and lets her in to see Troy then Mathias will revise his earlier judgment of her. He thinks the trip to the prison will be a waste of time but he calls the prison and sets up an appointment for Sabia and he to meet with Warden Django the next day.

Much to Mathias' surprise the warden seems to take Sabia seriously and he agrees to her meeting with Troy. He and Mathias will serve as chaperones.

Sabia walks down the corridor towards Troy's cell to a chorus of prisoner's whistles and catcalls. She is wearing her handmade kangaroo skin boots. They click against the gray floor making a sound that no kangaroo ever made. She is holding a shopping bag as well as her briefcase. The shopping bag is made of canvas and has a pattern of traditional Aboriginal designs in red and purple. It was a present from Rose. Sabia is nervous and excited. Mathias and Warden Django walk with her.

Troy hides the rope he has been working on as he hears all the noise outside. Cling! The key opens not only his cell door but a rush of memories for Troy as Sabia steps in - carefully - as if she were walking across an outback creekbed. Mathias follows her in with Warden Django. The warden is waiting to see if there is any sort of recognition of Sabia by Troy.

Against his better judgment he has decided to give Sabia one chance to meet Troy. The warden is watching Troy's face which registers the absolute disbelief of someone confronted with a ghost.

"It's been a long time, Sabia." He gets up off the bed. Sabia is frozen as a piece of stone. Troy moves to her, hugs her. Sabia almost collapses but he is strong, supporting her. She drops the bags. "It's all right, little sister. I'm here." He spreads his open hand on her face as if she's not real - just a mirage he's trying to touch. Their tears mingle together like a sudden rush of water in an outback river after a thunderstorm has broken a dry spell. They hold each other TIGHT! Warden Django exchanges a glance with Mathias. They will leave them to talk. "You have five minutes," he says as he shepherds Mathias from the cell. The warden and Mathias wait outside leaving the cell door open.

"You didn't do it," says Sabia. It's a statement, not a question.

"No, Sabia, you know I wouldn't do anything like that."

"Then who did it? I can see that you know who did it......why are you protecting them?

"He's just a scared kid."

"Troy, they could execute you. You're not going to be killed for someone else. I won't allow it. I couldn't lose you again."

Troy takes a deep breathe. How is he going to explain this to Sabia? He doesn't reply.

"He might be a scared kid, but he's a killer too. Don't forget that."

"Sabia, you don't understand. He just got caught up in something that he couldn't control."

"That's called life, Troy. You make your choices."

"He didn't have the luxury of making a choice. I'm telling you Sabia, he was forced into this."

"How do you even know him?"

Troy ignores her question. "How did you find me? I didn't think I'd ever see you or Mum again."

"Our mother told me you were overseas and then we saw you on the news."

"You found our mother. Where is she?"

"She wants me to bring you home. You've got to live, Troy. "You can't let yourself die here."

"What happened to you... after they took us? Do you still have that goanna I gave you?"

Sabia fishes it out of her briefcase. "I always carry this with me. I didn't even remember where I'd got it but I could never seem to throw it away. Just recently I started to remember what happened."

Troy takes the wooden goanna from her, looking at it as if he is seeing it again that day thirty years ago. "I didn't get a chance to finish it."

"I found her. Rose. Well, she found me. She says she's going to die. She wants to see you one last time. I've come to take you home before it's too late."

"Sabia, you might not be able to take me home. Don't get your hopes up. You might not be able to save me."

Sabia smiles. "Actually I need you to save me."

"Eh?" Troy is puzzled.

"I've got leukaemia."

"No." Troy wants to deny what he is hearing. He rubs Sabia's arm, disbelieving.

"Rose and I weren't a match and even if we were she's too sick to stand it. You're my last hope." Sabia looks down at the bag at her feet. "I've brought you a present. Sit down." Troy sits on the bed. Sabia removes his sneakers. Then she opens up the bag and pulls out a shoebox. She takes a pair of kangaroo skin boots out of the box.

"What's this? You've been watching too many westerns."

"Westerns?" queries Sabia.

"You think I'm one of those old western heroes and I'm going to die with my boots on," says Troy with a smile.

"That's the worst joke I've ever heard," says Sabia smacking Troy's knee. "These are handmade kangaroo skin boots. I bought them to remind you of our past. The kangaroo is our Aboriginal totem."
Sabia does up the buckle and Troy holds up one booted foot to admire. "We are strong people, Troy. We're like the kangaroo. We have 70,000 years of life in our veins. You can't die here.

"I'm going to take you home, whatever it takes. They stole 30 years from us. We might not have another 30 years."

"Sabia, there's just one thing I want you to promise me."

"Sure. Anything."

Troy holds the other kangaroo skin boot. "Don't you ever call me Skippy."

Sabia smacks his hand - lightly. The boot drops on to the concrete floor. It bounces - just like a kangaroo would. Troy looks at the boot, then at Sabia. "You're right, Sabia. They are kangaroo."

SABIA - USA

Later that night Mathias and Sabia are in a bar waiting for Fox. The door opens and Fox enters. Mathias introduces Fox to Sabia. "If Fox can't find that kid, no-one can."

"Well I found him."

"So what did he say?" asks Sabia and Mathias at the same time.

"Not much."

Sabia is anxious to see him. "Where is he? I must talk to him."

"Fraid not," says Fox.

"Look, wherever he is, I'll go there," says Sabia. "Whatever he wants, I'll get it. I'm not going to let Troy die here."

Fox leans in close to Sabia as if he thinks he will be overheard. "It's not good news."

"What?"

"I found him all right - in the morgue. Someone didn't want that kid to talk."

Mathias' eyes flash hot anger. 'Black Jack!' he thinks but he doesn't say anything to Fox and Sabia who is distraught. "How are we going to help Troy now?"

SUZY – USA

Mrs Lopez has applied to foster Suzy who is ready to leave hospital. As they finish packing Suzy's things, Mrs Lopez starts to take the bandage off the stuffed rabbit that Troy had bought Suzy.

"Your bunny's arm is better now too," she tells Suzy who looks worried.

"How is Troy going to find me?" she asks.

"Don't worry. Troy knows you are coming home with me and he lives just around the corner from us."

At last Suzy relaxes and smiles.

TROY – US PRISON

Troy and Joey meet up again in the exercise yard. Joey is curious about Troy's plans for himself. "I saw you working in your cell last night."

"Oh yeah," says Troy, very guarded, not wanting to give anything away.

"Looked to me like you were working on a rope."

"That so," says Troy.

"Don't use it too soon," says Joey. "Wait for developments."

"What developments?" asks Troy, puzzled about Joey's comment.

"Just wait, Bro," says Joey as he walks back inside.

MATHIAS - USA

For the first time in a long time Mathias is having an attack of conscience. In fact this is the first time in a long time that he has started to feel alive again and he does not want to lose this feeling.

It is early evening and he is working on Troy's case. He is totally absorbed in what he is doing. A half open bottle of Johnny Walker sits ignored on his desk. Suddenly there is a knock at the door. "Come in," says Mathias, looking up. It's too late for regular visitors so he steels himself for another visit by Black Jack. He half rises out of his chair but stops when he sees Cheyenne and Keesha enter.

After the introductions, Cheyenne tells Mathias about Jason and Black Jack and Keesha seeing Black Jack shoot Jason. A slow smile starts to spread across Mathias' face. Maybe this case is about to come alive and Black Jack will reap his just reward.

TROY – US PRISON

When the prison has finally quietened down for the night, Troy tests his knotted rope on the bars. One of the knots unravels and pulls away. His arm is flung backwards and hits the wall. As he rubs his arm he hears muffled voices and then a shadowy movement goes past his window as a large bundle is thrown off the roof. There's a loud noise as the bundle hits an obstacle below and an unholy scream of terror. Guards rush to the site. Impaled on the razor wire fence is the guard who administered a beating to Troy. He won't be beating any more prisoners.

MATHIAS – USA

Later that night Mathias is still working on Troy's case. It's late, very late, too late for clear thinking. Mathias has his old friend Johnny Walker with him but even this friend has deserted him tonight bringing him no solace, no comfort and no forgetting. He looks at the bottle - it's still half full. He makes his decision. The actions he is about to take will need clear thinking. He pours the contents of the bottle into the waste paper bin. Taking a very fancy Statue of Liberty lighter off his desk - a gift from a time when clients were still grateful for his talents - he drops the flame into the bin. Whoosh! The flame almost singes his eyes and hair but, anticipating the flame, he has pulled his head back. He stares mesmerized into the metal bucket as the flames gradually subside.

ROSE - AUSTRALIA

Rose is worried about Sabia and Troy. She has tried several times to call Sabia and left messages at her hotel. Today she woke up very early and walked the two miles to the phone box without stopping for breakfast. She is determined to reach Sabia today and find out what is happening with Troy. Her persistence has paid off and she is at last talking to Sabia from the most isolated telephone booth in the world. It is a telephone box by the side of Great Northern Highway. Stretching north and south is the highway with not even a tree to relieve the landscape.

"When are you and Troy coming home, Sabia?" asks Rose.

"How are you?" Sabia is worried about Rose.

"Don't you worry about me. I'm just happy that you found Troy. I'll be well again just as soon as you come home."

"We'll be there soon," says Sabia, hopefully.

TROY – US PRISON

After the death of the guard, the prison is on lockdown. Prisoners are confined to their cells while the warden undertakes an inquiry. Troy uses the time to work on his rope. He wants it ready to use as soon as possible. At the back of his mind he feels that there is little chance of him getting out of prison and he is becoming depressed about the future for Sabia and their mother. Troy has always hated to feel helpless but as the days go on he feels more and more helpless not just for himself but for the two people he most loves.

CHEYENNE – USA

On the day of Jason's funeral Keesha helps Cheyenne walk to the graveside. The crowd is small and Cheyenne is disappointed that more people aren't there to say a final farewell to her loving son. She thinks again about his last words: "I love you Mom" and she stumbles as she gets closer to the burial plot. First she lost Analie and now Jason. What is there left for her? Maybe if she had had a different husband her world and the world they could have provided for the children would have been better. She is grateful to have Keesha's help and she is concerned about the life she has been leading. After the funeral she plans to ask Keesha to move in with her so they can look after each other.

MATHIAS – USA

It is another late night. This time Mathias is not alone in his office. Fox is wiring him up with a listening device which he connects to the transmitter in a G-string tucked under Mathias's private parts. Needless to say Mathias is a bit touchy about what is going on. "Eh, take it easy, Fox. That's a bit personal down there."

Fox continues. "Don't worry. I could wire up a mother's breasts and her baby could still suck milk out of them."

"You don't have to do this, you know," says Mathias.

"Bullshit! I'm not doing this for you, I'm doing this for her."

Mathias is surprised. "For Sabia? But you only met her once."

"A woman like her, you only have to meet once."

"You old fox, pardon the pun. You're in love with her."

"Any man who meets her would be in love with her. She's got that revolutionary energy," says Fox as he finishes wiring Mathias.

"Revolutionary energy? What do you mean?"

"Women like her cause revolutions. Women like her are a pain in the bum. They're fighters! You see them coming with that revolutionary gleam in their eyes. The smoke trails behind them and you know you've got a revolutionary woman after you."

Mathias is even more surprised at hearing this from Fox. "I've never heard you talk about a woman like this before. So what are you going to do about it?"

"Nothing!"

"Nothing! How can you let her go when you feel like that?"

Fox has finished wiring up Mathias, who relaxes. "Exactly because I feel like this."

"Maybe that's the best thing, anyway, with things being how they are," says Mathias.

"What do you mean 'things being how they are'?" quizzes Fox.

"She may be a revolutionary woman but she's a sick revolutionary."

"Sick? What kind of sick?"

"She has leukemia. She's hoping her brother is a match so he can be her bone marrow donor."

Fox sits down suddenly as if the wind has been knocked out of his chest. Mathias is alarmed. He's never seen Fox so shocked. "You all right, Bro?" Fox doesn't speak for some time. Then he picks up his bag and gets up. "Let's go, we've got work to do."

BLACK JACK – USA

Across town Black Jack is snoring. He has one arm over his wife. The jangling of the phone is a harsh reality. He fumbles, then finally gets the receiver to his ear. Still half asleep he growls into the phone. "Yeah." His late night caller is Mathias.

"This has gone too far," says Mathias to Black Jack. We've got to talk." Black Jack agrees to meet Mathias in 30 minutes at Murphy's Bar, actually out the back in the carpark. Black Jack's wife stirs. "Go back to sleep. I gotta tie up some loose ends." He picks up his pistol, checks the clip to see that it is fully loaded. "No guts, no glory," he says to himself.

Mathias sits in the front seat of his car which is parked at a crooked angle in the alley. There's a reason for his bad parking. He has a clear view of anyone coming down the alley on foot or by car. He's smoking again - for the first time in five years. The lighter shows his face to any onlookers and that's the idea. He wants to lull Black Jack into a feeling of power and superiority. That's when people make mistakes.

Black Jack walks swiftly down the alley looking back over both shoulders. He's feeling pissed off. He was just getting up the energy to have a second shot at his wife. The last thing he wanted was to be dragged out of bed for this punk crooked lawyer. Still, a few minutes to make sure he gets the message and he can go back and wake her up and get to work. He slides into the front seat of Mathias' car. "What's so urgent that you dragged me out of bed?"

Mathias affects an attitude of simmering outrage. "You set me up. I don't like being set up."

"Listen asshole, you set yourself up. You're the one with the bad credit rating."

"This isn't about me. You wanted your partner dead and somehow you roped in that kid Troy's protecting."

"Yeah, isn't he something? He's gonna fry for that kid. What a loser! I shoulda done it myself. I shoulda known you never send a boy to do a man's job."

"Your partner knew about your rackets. But why kill him now - he'd kept quiet all this time."

"Internal affairs. He was going to talk to them. Silly fuck - he warned me first."

"Killing a cop is heavy stuff for a kid. How'd you get him to do it."

"Told him I'd rape his mother."

"Nice."

"Stupid kid believed me."

"And then you killed the kid."

"Had to when that other fuck got involved. He wasn't supposed to be there. I had it all worked out. Motherfucker! He screwed things up."

"You're a charmer, you know, a real charmer."

"I told you not to fuck with me. You get him to plead guilty or you're a dead man." Black Jack pulls out his gun to emphasize his point but another gun appears - like the disconnected hand of God. There's a loud Bang! But it's not the noise from a gun. It is Fox mimicking a gun as he leans through the window. Black Jack is startled, then he slumps forward, losing consciousness. Mathias grabs Black Jack's gun and Fox puts his gun back in his pocket. Fox grins at Mathias as he leans through the window. "You get all the gory details?"

"You can bet my balls on that," says Mathias. He starts to shake Black Jack who is slumped down in his seat. "Geez! You didn't really kill him, did you?"

"Guess he fainted," says Fox who is pushed aside as two plain clothed detectives stick their heads through the window. Seeing Black Jack out cold one of them says: "What the fuck? He better not be dead."

Fox blows on his fingers. "Just worked a bit of Vietnam magic on him. He'll wake up in about an hour."

"Did you get everything?" asks Mathias.

"Sure did. That bastard came through loud and clear," says one of the detectives.

Mathias grins. "He was so cocky, he didn't even think to look for a wire."

"What's next?" asks Fox sliding into the passenger seat as Black Jack is taken away.

"A visit to the DA's office," says Mathias.

"So you think you'll be able to spring Sabia's brother?" asks Fox.

"With what we got that black-hearted bastard to admit to tonight. And with what Keesha will be telling the DA tomorrow, he should be free by lunchtime – well a couple of days should do it."

SABIA – USA

The next morning Sabia and Mathias are ushered into the District Attorney's office. Mathias is anxious to start the process to drop the murder charge against Troy and have him released. He doesn't even wait to sit down as the D.A. offers him a chair.

"So you've got the tape. You've got Black Jack's confession. How soon will you be able to process the paperwork and have Troy released?"

"Now, hold up just a minute Counselor," says the D.A. "You know as well as I do that the tape is inadmissible in court."

"Of course I know that but you've seen Keesha's statement. She saw Black Jack shoot Jason."

Patiently the D.A. says: "Yes, but she didn't see Jason shoot Sargeant Strong. Your boy still had the blood and the gun on him."

"But you've heard Black Jack's confession. You know Troy didn't do it."

"It's not as easy as you would think to withdraw the charges. We'd need a written confession from Black Jack, not an inadmissible tape. It could be all bullshit. He could have sussed that you were wearing a wire and he made it all up. I doesn't prove anything.

"If I went into court right now with what you're trying to sell me I'd be laughed out of court. You've got to have something better than this."

Sabia's temper starts to rise but she knows how court officials operate from her experiences in Australia. She knows you have to get them on-side if you want anything from them otherwise they won't budge. "There's more to it, isn't there? You're not telling us everything."

The D.A. relaxes as Sabia smiles at him. "The mayor's been on my back. In fact I just got off the phone with him. This is a touchy time. Right before the election. He doesn't want a scandal – a rogue cop murdering civilians just before the election. He's leaning pretty hard on me to sit on this for a week or two until after the election."

Sabia's level of frustration almost pushes her to blurt out her annoyance but she holds herself in check. She smiles again at the D.A. "The thing is this is an emergency situation. You see I have leukaemia and I need a bone marrow transplant. My only hope is Troy. I need to get him out and take him back to Australia as soon as possible. I can't afford to wait a week or two – election or no election."

"I'm sorry to hear that but I'm not sure that I'll be able to change the mayor's mind."

"Please talk to him again," says Sabia. She flashes the D.A. another smile. "I would really appreciate your help" and she emphasizes "really".

As they leave the D.A.'s office they hear him ask his secretary to get the mayor on the phone.

"Climbing Mount Everest might have been easier," Sabia jokes to Mathias as they get in his car. "Let's go and see Troy and tell him how things stand. At least he will know that he is going to be released soon." But Sabia's upbeat mood soon dissipates when they reach the prison and find that it is on total lockdown because of the killing of the guard. "No visitors, no phone calls," the guard on duty tells them.

"Then I want to see the warden," Sabia says very determinedly.

"Not sure he'll want to see you," says the guard. He picks up the intercom phone receiver and dials the warden's office.

"Warden, that Australian lawyer lady is here and she wants to see you."

Sabia is astounded to learn that Troy has been taken to hospital. "Hospital? What happened? Is Troy alright?"

The warden is puzzled. "My office left a message on Mr Swinebourne's phone." He looks at Mathias, puzzled. "You didn't get the message?"

Mathias shakes his head. "What message?"

"I had a call first thing this morning from Professor Kander at Grand Central Hospital."

"What's that got to do with Troy?" asks Sabia.

"Your brother is on some list of people with rare blood types. The professor has a patient who urgently needs a transfusion and Washington was the only possible donor within 100 mile radius. He left under guard about an hour ago."

"What about the lockdown?" asks Mathias.

"The professor was very insistent so I gave permission. He'll be back later today the professor assured me."

"What hospital did you say he's at?" asks Sabia, getting up ready to leave.

"You can't go down there and interrupt the professor. You'd be better off coming back here later." But Sabia's not waiting for any professor.

She's off out the door with Mathias running to keep up. As they get in his car she turns on him. "Why don't you check your bloody phone messages?"

As they park in the visitor's carpark at the hospital, Fox runs over to their car. "Where the hell have you been? He's waiting for you?"

"What are you talking about?" asks Mathias and Sabia at the same time.

"I left a message on your phone this morning," says Fox. "Didn't you get it?"

Mathias gives Sabia a look. "Don't start." Then he turns to Fox. "What's this all about?"

Fox talks quickly as he ushers them through the back entrance and up the stairwell to the ward so that the prison guard will not see Mathias or Sabia. "He's a mate from Vietnam."

"Who?" asks Sabia.

"Oh now he's a professor, back then he was just a grunt doctor doing triage."

"And?" asks Mathias, still wondering what this is all about.

"He owes me one. So he's going to do the test on Troy and Sabia and see if Troy is a match. If he is, he'll do the transfusion right here."

"Here!" says Sabia. "Now?"

"That's what I've been trying to tell you. Wish you'd pick up your phone messages once in a while, Bro." He winks at Mathias and gives Sabia a huge grin.

"Fox – you sly dog." Mathias' smile lights up the corridor. Sabia gives Fox a beaming smile as they walk into the ward.

"Where've you been little sister?" asks Troy looking very pleased with himself.

Mathias and Fox wait in the professor's office off

to the side of the ward while Professor Kander has Sabia prepped for the test.

Sabia quickly tells Troy about the latest developments with Black Jack and their visit to the DA. She says she is bringing as much pressure to bear as she can to have the charge against Troy dropped and him released. While they wait for the lab to do a rush job on the results Sabia asks about how Professor Kander and Fox know each other.

"So you were in Vietnam together?" she prods.

"It wasn't just a case of being there at the same time," says the professor. "Fox saved my life. Actually not just mine – there were about 25 people in that tent. They're all alive today thanks to his courage."

"What happened?" asks Sabia with Troy keenly interested in someone else's experiences in the same war that he still has nightmares about.

"They'd brought in a lot of casualties and we were in the middle of triaging them when someone threw a hand grenade in. Fox had just walked into the tent to see if he could help us. He saw the grenade, picked it up and sprinted about 100 yards and then threw it into the river. It exploded in mid air above the river. Bravest thing I've seen."

"That's quite a story," says Sabia, not sure whether to believe it or not.

But Troy is puzzled about the day's events. "So how did you know about Sabia and me?"

"Fox rang me – well he got me out of bed at 4am this morning. Told me what was happening with you two. Of course I wanted to help. Anything for Fox."

"How did you organize the hospital and the tests and everything? asks Sabia.

"Officially you two are part of one of my research

projects so everything comes under that."

"Wow, that's amazing." Sabia is genuinely touched by his generosity.

"There's just one thing."

"What's that, Professor?" asks Troy.

"You'll have to pay the nurses for their time, but everything else is on me."

Mathias and Fox re-enter the ward. Sabia is at a loss for words. She wants to thank Fox but it seems like such a huge thing that he has arranged, that she is not sure how to thank him. Finally she decides to keep it simple but just as she is about to do it, Professor Kander comes in with the test results. Sabia holds her breath, desperate for it to be good news.

"Troy, I've just rung the warden and told him that we need to keep you here overnight as there are complications with my patient," says the professor.

Troy and Sabia look at each other and for a split second they don't understand. Then Sabia grins. "You're a match, Big Brother. He's telling us he's going to do the transfusion right here right now."

BLACK JACK – US HOLDING CELL

Black Jack is furious. That bastard lawyer! Wearing a wire! Black Jack is mad at himself that he didn't think about it at the time. He was so focused on leaning on Mathias that he wasn't expecting or even thinking about him wearing a wire. Not that it will be admissible in court anyway but no doubt it's the end of his career. By now internal affairs will have the tape. And, as if they were reading his mind, three internal affairs officers walk into the holding cell. At first Black Jack affects his usual arrogance denying everything but as the questioning progresses he realizes that the best he may be able to achieve is some kind of deal. The Internal Affairs officers are also under pressure from the mayor's office to achieve the best possible result quietly so the press doesn't get wind of the full extent of Black Jack's nefarious activities.

Black Jack has an uncanny ability to read people. That's what has made him so successful at extorting money from his marks. He knows that if he cooperates he may get a better result than he was expecting. The Internal Affairs lead officer makes it very plain to Black Jack that they have the incriminating tape. At first Black Jack appears to bluff. He knows it would be inadmissible in court but no-one wants this to end in court. Gradually he allows himself to be talked into a deal. He agrees that he will admit that he co-erced Jason in the killing of Sargeant Strong, he will admit to killing Jason, he will serve 15 years and he will be allowed to keep his police pension. Black Jack knows that he will probably not last long in prison even though he will be placed in isolation but his wife at least will be looked after and that is about the only decent thing that he has done in a very long time.

SABIA – USA

Sabia and Mathias go back to the DA's office trying to press for the release of Troy. The DA tells them that he was unsuccessful in having the Mayor agree to Troy's release before the election which is now a week away. Finally Sabia has had enough. "You get on the phone and tell that mayor that I am going to sue him personally for $50 million for wrongful arrest and wrongful imprisonment of Troy and, if I haven't heard by noon today that Troy is to be released, your famous mayor will be watching me on every news program in this city tonight. "Do I make myself clear?"

Mathias grins to himself thinking that Fox was right about Sabia. She certainly is a revolutionary woman. Sabia storms out of the DA's office as she says over her shoulder. "I will ring you at noon. You better have the right answer for me."

Mathias drives Sabia upstate on their way to the prison where Troy is waiting to hear the results of her second visit to the DA's office. At 11.30 am they park at a diner where they will call the DA exactly at noon. Sabia is anxious and Mathias tries to calm her nerves by asking her about her life in Australia.

"Do you have your own law practice or do you work for one of the big firms?"

"I run my own show so I can do pro bono work as well as paying cases," says Sabia.

"Who's looking after your clients while you've been here?"

"I have several friends who are covering for me while I'm here."

Mathias thinks he'll move on to more personal information.

"You know I hardly know anything about you."

Sabia realizes what he is doing. "What do you want to know?"

"Well for instance, are you married, engaged, divorced, involved?"

Sabia laughs. "None of the above."

"Well that's a relief," says Mathias, grinning. "Why?"

"No reason, just wondering."

Sabia looks at her watch for the umpteenth time in

the last half hour. "It's time."

She's grinning as she comes back out of the telephone booth. "So he gave you the right answer," says Mathias. Sabia nods as she picks up her briefcase. "Let's go and get Troy."

But all is not as easy as Sabia was expecting. The warden is adamant that he will not release Troy while the prison is still on lockdown.

There has been no definitive result to his inquiry into the guard's death and he is not convinced that Troy was not involved. "Your brother might not have killed that policeman but he could have killed the prison guard."

"What!" says Sabia who is not even bothering to control her temper this time. "You must be insane. What possible reason could Troy have for killing a prison guard?"

"It's well known that he suffered a beating at the hands of the guard soon after he arrived."

"Look, what sort of prison are you running, Warden? A prison where prisoners get beaten up by guards. That will be a great story on the news. I can see it now: 'Warden admits prison guards are out of control. Prisoners suffer vicious beatings.' Come on Mathias, I'm off to see the Governor. He'll be very interested in this. So will the media when they find out that I'm dying and Troy is my only hope for survival and he's being illegally detained. This is going to be very, very expensive, Warden."

TROY – US PRISON

While Sabia and Mathias are on their way to see the Governor to argue for Troy's release, Troy is in the exercise yard of the prison grateful that the prisoners can at last exercise again even though the warden's inquiry is ongoing. Troy hated being cooped up. He sees Joey across the yard and can see that Joey is surprised to see him. "Word is you really are innocent. You didn't kill that cop. What are you still doing here?"

"The warden thinks I killed that guard. He heard about the beating the guard gave me. Thinks I retaliated."

"So he's not going to let you go? But didn't the DA withdraw the charges?"

"The warden's not satisfied that I've told him the truth. He doesn't believe that I don't know anything about that guard's death."

Joey grins. "Heard your sister creating all kind of mess. She's a tough one, tru dat."

Troy decides to appear to open up a bit more with Joey. "She's fighting for her life."

"What do you mean?"

"Sabia's got leukemia. She needs me out so I can be her bone marrow donor – to save her life."

"Heavy stuff, man. You got a lot going on – you and your sister."

Troy is almost sure that Joey either killed the guard or knows who did. He can't ask him directly but he feels that if he loads the dice heavily Joey might feel obliged to respond to the warden's inquiry.

"And she's also worried about our mother," says Troy.

"Your mother's here too?" asks Joey.

"No, she's back in Australia. She's very sick. My sister wanted to take me home to see her before she dies."

"Mega heavy," says Joey shaking his head. "Your ma, huh."

"Yes," says Troy as he walks away.

Joey thinks about what a solid citizen his own mother was. "Gotta do something," he says to himself.

A little later the warden is surprised to receive a request for a meeting by prisoner Joey Sanchez. In all the years that he has known Joey he has never known him to ask for a meeting. He is even more surprised to hear what Joey has to say.

Joey is infamous for being closed mouth. He's never been known to volunteer any information on anything to do with prison activities so Warden Django is in two minds about whether to believe him. On closer questioning of Joey he realizes that Joey is telling the truth for once in his life. He has details about the guard's death that no-one else was privy to. Joey may not have acted alone – although he says he did – but in any case he was definitely up on the roof when the guard was thrown off. Joey is adamant that Troy had nothing to do with it.

The warden is puzzled about Joey's offer to incriminate himself in something as serious as the death of a prison guard especially when Joey knows it will add serious time to his sentence.

"Why are you so concerned about Washington?" he asks.

"Warden I've met some real scumbags in my life, in my line of work. Don't often meet someone real decent, ya know. I wasn't there for Ma when she died. He should be there for his Ma."

SABIA – USA

Sabia is not sure she will be able to get to see the Governor but she is certainly going to make the effort. She was in a real tear when they left the prison and Mathias is quiet as he drives her to Albany to the Governor's office. He keeps an eye on Sabia and notices that she has finally calmed down. "Look, I have a friend in the Governor's office. If you really want to see the Governor I should call him and give him a heads up. It won't go down well if we just arrive and you start demanding to see him."

Sabia can see the sense in Mathias' plan so they pull in to a gas station to make the phone call. As Sabia goes inside to get some coffee she reminds Mathias to check the messages on his office phone at the same time. "OK, OK," he agrees, slightly annoyed that she is still rubbing his nose in his overlooking his messages at a time when it was urgent for she and Troy that he had checked them. As she comes out of the gas station she notices that Mathias has parked the car the wrong way – it is pointing back towards the city.

"What's going on?" Mathias holds the car door open for her. "You can forget the Governor."

"Why?" asks Sabia starting to feel irritated. She is hoping that he is not playing games with her, she is not in the mood.

"We're going to pick up Troy. The warden had left a message on my phone. Troy's out."

For Sabia, travelling the distance back to the prison seems to take forever. Finally they are there and Troy is waiting for them outside the gates. Sabia's smile is big enough to light up the sky as she and Mathias drive up next to Troy. She jumps out and hugs him.

"Finally," she says.

"Yes, finally, Little Sister. Finally," says Troy.
"Let's go home to Rose."

SUZY – USA

Mrs Lopez is in her bodega putting icecreams in the freezer. Suzy is helping her by pulling icecream sandwiches out of the box and handing them to her when she suddenly looks up at the front door, drops the icecreams and squeals as she runs to the man who has just come into the shop.

"Troy! It's really you." And Suzy starts to cry.
"Yes, Suzy, it's really me." He picks her up. She hugs him tightly.

"I thought I would never see you again."

"Well here I am in one piece but if you hug me so tightly I'll be in several pieces on the floor." He pinches her nose. "Have you been good for Mrs Lopez."

"Yes, she's been a great help to me," says Mrs Lopez, coming out from behind the counter and giving Troy a hug and a kiss as he puts Suzy back down.

"Well in that case…" and Troy reaches into his backpack and pulls out a package. Handing it to Suzy he says: "I found some friends for you."

Suzy excitedly unwraps the parcel. She pulls out two stuffed toy kangaroos – one black, one white. She hugs them both. "They're beautiful. Thank you Troy, I love them."

"Don't hug them too tight," says Troy.

"Why not?" asks Suzy, looking puzzled.

"Because you might squash the joey."

"What joey?" asks Suzy.

"Where do you normally find a joey kangaroo?" asks Troy.

"............ in the pouch," says Suzy, feeling inside the pouch of the white kangaroo. Her fingers can feel a little lump which she scrabbles and gets out. It is a tiny, brown joey kangaroo. She is delighted. "Now I have an Australian family too," says Suzy. "Well you need to name them," says Mrs Lopez. Suzy screws up her face examining the toys. Suddenly she says: "Kanga, Katerina and Kiss Kangaroo" all in one breath. "They're my new Australian family. And you of course, Troy. Mrs Lopez – Aunty Lou - told me that you were born in Australia so you are Australian and American. And you're also my American family – with Aunty Lou."

"So now that you have two families you won't miss me while I'm away," says Troy.

Suzy looks unhappy. "Oh no Troy, you're not going away again?"

"Just to Australia. To see my mother."

"You have a mother in Australia?" asks Suzy.

"Yes, and I haven't seen her for a very long time."

"You must go and see your mother," says Suzy. "You will come back though, won't you?"

"Of course I'll come back. Now there's someone I want you to meet." And Troy goes out to the car and brings in Sabia. Suzy and Sabia click immediately and Suzy wants to know if Sabia can be her sister too as well as Troy's so Suzy's family continues to grow.

Just then Mathias and Fox drive up and park outside the bodega. As Fox enters he winks at Sabia who grins back at him.

"We thought you might need a ride to the airport," says Mathias.

"Hey," says Fox, nudging Mathias. "Aren't you

going to introduce me to this young lady?"

"Oh, sure. This is young Suzy. I told you about her," says Mathias.

Fox shakes Suzy's finger as her hands are full of kangaroos. "Very pleased to meet you, Miss Suzy. Are you going to introduce me to your friends?"

Suzy is so happy she's like a dog with two tails as she introduces her new toys to Fox and Mathias.

"You know you may be able to help me, Ms Suzy," says Fox as Mrs Lopez looks on, happy that Suzy is the center of attention. Suzy smiles at him.

"Anything for a friend of Troy's ... and Sabia's," she adds quickly, not wanting Sabia to feel left out. "What can I help you with?"

"Well I had an idea the other day. You see I live in a forest."

"Are there lots of animals there?" asks Suzy.

"Yes and birds too and fish – there's a lake."

"Do you ever see rainbows on the lake?"

"As a matter of fact I get rainbows almost every day. In fact I call it Rainbow Lake."

"Sounds wonderful but what can I do?"

"Well I wanted your opinion actually," says Fox.

"About what?" asks Suzy, really enjoying the banter with Fox.

"See, it occurred to me that my forest and my lake might make a really nice summer camp for children and I wondered if you think that would be a good idea."

"Sounds really nice. I'm sure kids would love it," says Suzy. "I know I would. We could all be called Rainbow Riders."

"Well I'd have to build the huts and such so it won't be ready for a few months but when it is you'd be welcome to come – Rainbow Rider - and of course

Mrs Lopez could come too."

Mathias is astounded at Fox's idea. Apart from his music gigs at the bar, it's the first time Fox has actively planned interaction with people on a larger scale. Mathias looks at Sabia. Maybe this revolutionary woman is having a subtle but strong effect on Fox. He is pleased about it.

Fox turns to the others. "I thought we could all do it together," he says.

"It's a great idea but it will be a bit hard for me to have any involvement from Australia," says Sabia.

"Maybe you could come over during the summer for at least part of the time," Fox says hopefully.

"It would be a nice break," says Sabia.

At the airport Mathias pulls up outside the International Departures area. While he waits in the driver's seat Fox gets their luggage out and puts it on the airport sidewalk. Troy says goodbye to Mathias and then turns to pick up their luggage to see Fox giving Sabia a very strong kiss. Troy turns back to Mathias and gives him a "thumbs up" sign.

SABIA AND TROY – AUSTRALIA

Sabia and Troy are in identical hospital beds. Professor Kander's transfusion started the process for Sabia and it is being continued now that they are back in Perth. As Sabia reads through some legal files, Troy writes a letter to Suzy. He suddenly looks over at Sabia and smiles. "I know why you got sick, Sis."

"Oh you do, heh? Why then, you just tell me Old Wise Big Brother."

"Yep, I know. You got sick so you could use it as an excuse to keep me here in Australia, so I wouldn't have to go back."

"That so?"

"I reckon."

Sabia grins at him. "Well it worked. You're here. Anyway Troy, you're wrong."

"Wrong? About what?"

"About the boots."

"The boots?"

"You didn't die with your boots on."

"And neither will you," says Troy.

Just then Madeline comes into the room. She is carrying a cup of coffee. "I was just thinking."

"What?"

"They'll never be able to separate you two again. Wherever you go from now on you will be carrying part of each other inside you."

"Mum, that's very poetic," says Sabia.

Troy puts on a mock serious face. "Just don't you do anything that I wouldn't do."

Sabia is equal to the charge. "Or?????"

"Or I'll train my cells to just get up and leave!"

Sabia bursts out laughing.

ROSE - AUSTRALIA

Back at Python Pool Rose is swimming.

Sabia and Troy are out of hospital and have travelled north to visit Rose and for Troy to reconnect with his "sit down country." They are standing at the water's edge. Rose looks up at them, her tears start to fall. She can't speak. All she can think of is how for thirty years she had dreamt of this moment and it is finally here. Troy doesn't hesitate. He walks fully clothed into the water and hugs his mother. "Hello Mum. I'm sorry I've been gone so long." Sabia joins them in the pool. "How are you Rose?" Rose hugs Sabia. "Good girl. You bought your brother home. Thank you. Now I can die happy."

"Don't talk about dying, Rose. We've just got here."

Over campfire coffee Troy tells Rose about the Washingtons and his life in New York. He mentions his time in Vietnam but doesn't go into detail. And he talks enthusiastically about Fox's plans for the Rainbow Riders Children's Camp. He is looking forward to working with Fox to get the camp up and running.

Later that day the three of them are fishing in Python Pool just like Rose had been hoping for these long, long years.

Then it is time to catch up on the old familiar places as Rose, Sabia and Troy walk through the bush to the lilypond.

Suddenly Rose sees two kangaroos sitting on their haunches, waiting. They look almost like an animal welcoming committee for Sabia and Troy. The three of them freeze and quietly watch the roos.

It is as if the clock has turned back thirty years and Sabia and Troy are those two young children who played so happily in the bush with not a worry in the world. After a few minutes the roos hop off into the bush. The re-united family continue on to the waterlily pond. As they splash about, Troy's attention is on something in the bush when he hears Sabia call out. "Troy, help me! Rose is in trouble. She's sinking." Sabia is trying to help her up. Troy reaches them and carries Rose out of the pool and lays her down in the shade of a palm tree. Rose's eyes are closed. Sabia leans in close to check on her breathing. "What is it?" asks Troy.

"I think it's her emphysema. We'll have to drive over to Millstream Station and call the Flying Doctor."

As Sabia cradles Rose's head on the back seat of the car Troy drives as fast as he dare to Millstream Station. The owner of the station immediately recognizes a medical emergency. He helps Troy carry Rose into their living room while his wife calls the Flying Doctor Service on their two-way radio.

The Flying Doctor radio operator relays the information to Doctor Joyce Coogan who is the pilot and who has just dropped off a patient at a station property nearby. "Joyce, can you divert and pick up a patient at Millstream?"

"What are the symptoms?" asks Dr Coogan.

"Sorry Doc. I haven't got much detail I'm afraid. The patient collapsed and is having trouble breathing. That's all I've got."

In the fading light of dusk the Royal Flying Doctor Service plane lands at Millstream Station. Troy carries Rose out to the plane where she is helped aboard by Dr Coogan and nurse Stacey.

Sabia climbs on board with her. There isn't room for Troy so he will drive down to Perth.

Dr Coogan examines Rose. "What happened?"

"I was in the water swimming with her when she suddenly couldn't breathe and started to pass out."

"Do you know if she is allergic to anything?" asks Dr Coogan. "Not that I know of," answers Sabia.

Darkness has descended so the station owner and Troy light bonfires along the runway so the plane will have enough light to take off safely. Sabia is worried about Rose and also about Troy. "Please drive carefully. I know you will be racing but please be careful. Promise you won't drive like a bat out of hell."

"Don't worry no bat's gunna catch me." In the light from the bonfires the plane speeds down the strip and takes off into the night. Troy gives a salute and waves at the disappearing plane.

As Troy drives south along the highway the tenseness in his face shows how worried he is. Suddenly the headlights of his car pick out a roo a little way down the road. It looks like it's about to jump across the road into the path of Troy's car. He shouts through the windscreen at the roo. "Don't! Don't even think about it, Roo." The roo seems frozen at the edge of the road. It doesn't even move as Troy's car passes it. He relaxes a little. "Well that seemed to work pretty well."

It is midday the next day and Sabia is dozing in a chair by Rose's bed as Troy arrives. He comes quietly through the door trying not to wake either of them. Sabia opens her eyes as soon as she hears him. "You must have scared the hell out of those bats."

"They're still batting their wings trying to catch me." He bends down and kisses her. Trying to keep things light, he says: "Have a nice flight?"

"Good view," says Sabia.

"So what did the doctors say?"

"They've done some tests."

Dr Coogan and Nurse Stacey come in. "We're just knocking off. How's the patient?"

Troy is puzzled by the phrase. "Knocking off?"

"Knocking off work. Going home," Dr Coogan enlightens him.

"Can't you tell us how she is?"

"Dr Yin will be in as soon as she's got the results of the tests. "Shouldn't be long."

Thanks for everything," says Sabia.

"Hey, it's all in a day's work," says Dr Coogan. Nurse Stacey chimes in: "Just part of the service."

Rose wakes up. She smiles at them both. "Thank you for taking such good care of me." She suddenly sees Troy. "Oh, you're here. I'm glad."

An hour later Sabia is reading a magazine while Troy is asleep in the armchair. Dr Yin comes in with charts in her hand. "How are you feeling, Rose?"

"I can breathe better."

"What's wrong Doctor?"

"It's your emphysema. It's got worse, I'm afraid. You haven't been taking your medicine have you?"

"Sorry, Doc. But I ran out so I was making bush medicine."

"We'll make you as comfortable as possible, Rose," says Dr Yin.

Troy and Sabia follow the doctor out into the corridor. "How bad is she?" asks Sabia.

"She doesn't have very long," says the doctor. She must have been suffering for some time."

"She wouldn't stay down here in Perth so she could be carefully watched by the doctors. So she must have run out of her medicine and has been treating herself with bush medicine," says Sabia.

"Well that can be helpful but I'm afraid your mother is in the last stages." Sabia grabs Troy's hand. The doctor continues. "You should start to say your goodbyes." Sabia and Troy go back inside to sit with Rose who has fallen asleep again.

One week later Sabia and Troy are back at Python Pool, this time without Rose. Sabia looks up to the sky as she takes an urn out of her bag. Troy holds out his hands and Sabia pours some of Rose's ashes into his hands. He sprinkles the ashes out over the water. Sabia holds the urn up to the sky and then tips it and sprinkles the rest of the ashes into the water.

From the hot red cliffs above the pool a snake comes sliding out along the rocks and slips silently into the water. As it enters the water a rainbow spreads across the pool.

And out across the spinifex-covered plains three Aboriginal dancers are dancing the kangaroo dance.

ABOUT THE AUTHOR:

Sally Squires was born in Perth, Australia. She is a traveler and her curiosity has seen her as a resident of Australia, the USA and Vietnam. She is passionate about writing and about encouraging other writers and to further that support she has initiated the Asia-Pacific Writing Awards. Details can be found at www.dragonzilla.com.

Her books for adults include:

SKIN OF THE KANGAROO
ALLIGATORS AND JACK NICHOLSON
NAPOLEON'S LAST NIGHT
SAUCY SALLY'S SALUBRIOUS SCRUMMIES
G'DAY MATE

Her children's books are:

MERMAIDS ARE COOL
NICK NOCK NACK
OZZ WOZZ
MICETRALIA
ANGELS WITH ATTITUDE

Sally's books and DVDs are available:
www.amazon.com
www.createspace.com
and from the publisher

Her websites are:

www.dragonzilla.com
www.messagefromamermaid.com
www.mermaidsarecool.com
www.nusefuse.com

You can email Sally at:
GDay1717@hotmail.com
ssquires1717@gmail.com

WE ARE ALL ONE

Made in the USA
Charleston, SC
11 January 2015